THE DEVIL'S GAME

Written by:

SHAWN 'JIHAD' TRUMP

Acknowledgments

First and foremost, I have to thank Allah (God) for making everything in life possible. Wahida Clark, thank you for being patient. I pushed the limit and went well beyond the deadlines you set forth. It's so much harder writing in the streets than when I'm behind them walls. My wife Tinesha and my daughters Shainiece and Shaianna. I love you all. You guys have put up with so much and have still stood beside me. The three of you are the glue that holds my life together. My babies mama, Tracy, you have done an amazing job raising our girls, and I am grateful that we are friends. Alicia, we have maintained a friendship after the storm, and you pulled through and really helped me out with the typing when I didn't have time. To my mother and father. Life hasn't always been the greatest, but yinz did your best. Thank you for everything. To my in-laws. Thank you for always supporting me and not turning your back on me. You never judged me and that is appreciated.

To those who stood by me while I was down, I love you. Sabrina, Dee, Jonny, Tawnia, Tracey S. and Steph. Your letters and friendship means a lot.

Dave (Big Country). You deserve your own paragraph along with a few others. We been doing this for years. We go thru ups and downs like brothers. We argue, don't see eye to eye, then drink some Henny and forget about it. You always have my back, even if it involves tough love. Thank you for everything.

Gabe, you are my brother. We stand back to back through any adversity. Nothing more needs to be said.

Punchy, cuzo we are always there for one another no matter what. I love you, family.

Dwuan, my B-More brother. It goes without saying. You know what it is with us. What's mine is yours. We just got to stay out the strip clubs. Nothing good ever comes out of us and strip clubs, bro.

Terrance Triplett. I love you, man. It kills me that you are stuck in there. The same prison I just left they threw you right in to take my place. Man, we did our thing. Until you get out here I'm holding it down. Words can't explain how much I value your presence in my life. You are 100% real at all times. I still remember getting you drunk on your wedding night and you not going home till 4 a.m. But that's what we do, right? I miss you out here.

To my other comrades out here with me. Drekie, Shep, Banes, Sayquan, Bell, Bum, Tim R, Tim B, Chill, Meek, Young D, Spud, Montana, Hoss, Rod, Mike, Fran, Brice, JB, Kamal, Kimmi, Kristen, L, Tu, Russ, Rick H, Rick P, Yah Yah, and I can't forget Tuck, my main man from NY. We had a nice stretch in that law library. Thanks for letting me use you as a character in my book, bro.

To those stuck in that beast. Clay and G Moorefield, As Salamu Alaikum. Big G, had you at the first book signing and we did it up with some Henny. I'll make sure you get a copy. Can't wait till lil bro gets home. Stay strong soldier. Bobby White, Sharanda Jones, Derrick Morris, Seth Ferranti, Booker, Michael Fernandez, Joseph Petaway, Brett Finsick, and all the other brothers stuck inside. If I forgot you it's not intentional.

CHAPTER 1

Y
o, I can't stand being on the run," said Chris as he focused on the Madden game, moving side to side as if he were running the ball himself.

"I feel you," replied his boy Quick, who sat next to him.

"Seriously, I don't be trusting none of these motherfuckers out here. Always want me to help them out, but talkin' shit behind my back. That's why I only fuck with you. 'Cause I know one of these faggots will put them people on me," Chris stated, pushing the buttons on the controller.

"Well, no matter what, I got your back," replied Quick.

"No doubt. That's why I make sure you're the one who's eating out here."

"Ugghh!" he grunted and paused the game after his quarterback got sacked. Frustrated, he threw the controller on the floor.

"Damn dawg, why you do that? I was about to score," Quick complained.

Chris jumped up and went to check the window, something he did on the regular. Although it was a beautiful summer day, being on the run and unable to enjoy kicking it outside with his homies or his girl, Misty only annoyed Chris. A warrant had been issued for his arrest, and the police were very familiar with him. One white face in a sea of black faces made Chris an easy target to spot. Therefore, he stayed inside, knowing he had left George Junior Republic (GJR), a juvenile detention facility in Pittsburgh, well before his time was up.

He looked at the cars parked on the street in front of the house, and then he turned from left to right, checking for foot traffic. Satisfied that the block was clear of any unfamiliar cars and faces, Chris plopped down on the couch back in front of the television.

Thirty-five minutes later, Quick and Chris's game ended. He had just beat Quick for the fifth time, and the two sat around bullshitting about life. Chris let Quick know that he was going to Florida with his girl Misty to start over.

"Florida? What the fuck you going down there for?"

"I'm tired of this bullshit up here, fam'. I need a clean slate. I got a fucking bull's-eye on my chest up here."

Quick started to protest, but his pager began to vibrate. "Let me call this dude back," he said, already thinking about the $1,000 he would be making off this lick.

After three rings, the man answered his phone. Quick paused to listen to the caller. "You tell me. You're the one who paged me. Remember?" he said.

After a ten second pause, Quick looked over at Chris and said, "Yo, I need four and a half for Manny."

"Cool," Chris said. He got up and walked into one of the two small rooms in the finished basement that Quick was kind enough to let him have. A couch and television furnished part of the area that posed as a living room, so it was almost as if they shared an apartment. Chris's room was extremely small and sat adjacent to the living room that was barely big enough for a bed and dresser. He could have gotten his own place, but why spend the money when he was trying to stay close to

Misty. Plus, staying with Quick was convenient, considering Quick was moving all his product. He spent most nights with Misty anyway, and only came over to Quick's house during the day while Misty was at school.

He opened a small safe in the corner of the room and took out a large freezer bag. After retrieving his digital scale from his dresser, he weighed out 125 grams of what he had nicknamed "jet fuel," due to its smell and potency. He then transferred it into a smaller bag and handed it to Quick.

"Good look, fam'," Quick said.

"You know how we do," Chris replied.

Quick turned and walked out the door. The streets were a jungle. Anytime he stepped outside he knew anything could happen. Between the task force, stickup boys, and the jealous haters, nobody could be trusted. An uneasy feeling rumbled in the pit of his stomach. Chris shook it off and went back to his room and lay down.

CHAPTER 2

Quick jumped into his red Ford Escort and started it up as the amp kicked on and Top Authority's "Tell it to My Nine" blasted through the speakers. Quick bobbed his head while reciting the lyrics.

As he drove, Quick thought about what he was going to do when Chris left and moved to Florida. He had a lot of plans based on the money he was making off his dealings with Chris. But unlike Chris, Quick never saved for a rainy day. He spent it as it came in, knowing Chris would front him whatever he needed. Reality was, if Chris left today, Quick wouldn't have much money to get more product. He would have to start stacking his money. Silently, he prayed that Chris would bless him by hooking him up with his connect, Jesus. Sometimes it irritated him that he was moving all the work and taking all the chances while Chris just sat around eating and fucking. He knew he had to suck it up though, because for now Chris was his lifeline. However, if the opportunity presented itself, he would move on Chris's laziness and trust.

Snapping back to reality, Quick pulled his car in front of Manny's house and jumped out. Manny stood outside waiting and slapped fives with Quick.

"Quick, what it do homie?" asked Manny as he took a seat on the porch. "Ma Dukes is inside."

Quick tossed Manny the Crown Royal bag and said, "$4, 500."

Manny looked inside the Crown Royal bag and then looked up at Quick. "Still $4,500? When you gonna show me some love?" he asked.

"You act like this shit is free. Shit, I'm paying $3,500, and you're getting it raw. I know you're gonna put something on it and still charge $1,200 a pop."

"I'm sayin' though—" Manny stated but was cut off.

"What the fuck you sayin'? You know the price when you call me. If you don't wanna pay it then holla at someone else," Quick snapped, irritated with Manny's need to always try and get a deal.

"Who the fuck you think you talkin' to?" Manny started to get in his feelings. He and Quick were cool and did business together, but they weren't friends. Quick had a foul mouth at times, and this wasn't the first time he rubbed Manny the wrong way. If it wasn't for the work being A-1, he would have been stopped fucking with him.

"I'm talkin' to you, motherfucker!" Quick nailed Manny with a solid punch in the mouth.

Quick had always been the aggressor and vicious with his hands. He spent his childhood in the boxing ring, but never developed any form of discipline. Ultimately, his trainer threw him out of the gym for fighting in the streets, which was sad because he had had a good chance at becoming a great fighter. Everyone told him he had a shot at the golden gloves, but it went in one ear and out the other. Quick was going to do what he wanted to do and that was that. Like many kids growing up in the hood, Quick chose the streets over his talent, and his boxing career went down the drain.

Manny stumbled but regained his balance as he reacted with a counter punch to Quick's jaw. The two men of equal proportion locked up and began to tussle on the porch. Ripping his shirt, Manny finally broke free and without hesitation, pulled a chrome plated .25 from his waist and placed the muzzle on Quick's head. Manny knew he didn't have a win straight up against Quick. With gun in hand, Manny's confidence blossomed.

"Talk that shit now, pussy," said Manny as he fought to control his breathing.

Quick froze as the steel pressed hard against his forehead. He didn't think Manny would buck. "G-g-go ahead with that shit, Manny," he said with caution.

"Go ahead with what, motherfucker? Where's all that gangsta shit now, pussy? You was quick to throw them hands, Quick," Manny said sarcastically.

Fear wouldn't allow Quick to get the words out. Plenty of gunplay took place in the 'hood, but this was the first time in Quick's life that it jeopardized him. He stared into Manny's eyes trying to think of a way out of his predicament, but Manny held all the cards.

"You's a stupid motherfucker. You ain't getting shit. As a matter of fact, go ahead and kick up that chain too, you punk motherfucker," Manny ordered.

Manny never liked stickup kids, but this was different. Quick had disrespected him in his house, and Manny wasn't going to tolerate it. Quick was going to suffer a loss and learn not to play with him.

Without hesitation, Quick took off the chain that hung around his neck. He wasn't going to buck. There was no way he was going to die over money he owed Chris. He would just be beat. Chris had enough money to accept the loss.

Seeing how easily compliant Quick was, Manny's heart grew to the size of a lion's. His words became stronger than steel. "As a matter of fact, take *all* that shit off," he demanded.

"What you mean take it off?" Quick asked, even though he knew what Manny was saying.

"You heard me, motherfucka. The jeans, the shirt, the shoes. Strip, pussy. I want all that shit." Manny now intended to not just rob Quick, but also humiliate him.

Quick somberly began removing his clothes before Manny's mom happened to look out on the two men. She walked out the door and screamed in shock, "Man-Man, what the fuck you think you're doing?"

Without allowing a second to pass, Quick used the distraction to his advantage. He turned and bolted off the porch toward his car. Manny ran to the edge of the porch and raised the pistol. Before he squeezed the trigger, his mom jumped on him and began wrestling for the firearm.

"Are you fucking crazy!" she shouted.

Not willing to be confrontational with his mother, Manny released the gun. He grabbed the Crown Royal bag that had fallen during the tussle and Quick's chain. Manny hung the chain around his neck, and walked off the porch headed straight to his ride. He drove off with a smile on his face as his mother hollered after him.

"Fuck Quick!" he said as he turned up the music, allowing his thoughts to drift away. He knew Quick wasn't about gunplay and Manny stayed strapped, so he wasn't worried.

CHAPTER 3

This motherfucker must think I'm a chump!" Quick shouted over and over, fuming as he drove home.

Pulling in front of his house, he ran inside and grabbed his gun from under his mattress.

"Chris! Yo Chris! Where you at?" he hollered.

Chris heard the commotion and jumped out of bed. When he walked into Quick's room, he noticed the pistol in his friend's hand.

"What the fuck's going on?" Chris asked.

"That nigga Manny just put the burner to my head and took the work! I'm about to go give him the business right now!" Quick shouted, too embarrassed to tell Chris the truth.

"What happened?" Chris asked, trying to digest everything.

"I went over there, and as soon as I walked in the house he put the burner to the back of my head. There was nothing I could do."

"Where's he at now?"

"I don't know. His mom interrupted shit and distracted him. If it wasn't for her, me and you probably wouldn't even be talking now. I just took off, but dude was trying to give it to me."

Damn! Chris thought. *Me and Manny always been cool . . . Manny don't know whose shit he just took.* Quick was Chris's man though, and if Manny crossed him he had to be dealt with. Plus, any dude that would just rob someone they were cool with for no reason was a grimy motherfucker.

"Chill out for now. I'll deal with Manny later. Don't nobody know I'm around. Let his punk ass think shit's sweet, and right before I go to Florida I'll crack his motherfuckin' head," Chris instructed.

"Fuck that. I need my money. I got shit to do. I can't stand a thousand dollar loss," Quick said.

Without thought, Chris reached into his pocket and withdrew a knot wrapped tightly in a rubber band. He peeled away five one hundred dollar bills and passed it to Quick. "I'll give you another five on the next flip."

"Good look, fam'," Quick said.

As Chris turned and walked back in his room, Quick hoped that he didn't try to holler at Manny. His lie turned out better than he thought. Not only did Chris promise to take care of Manny, but Quick got paid to get robbed. *Dumb motherfucker*, Quick thought regarding Chris.

When Chris got to his room, he turned on his music and tried to lay back and relax. Things didn't make sense, but he didn't have any reason not to trust Quick. They had been friends since grade school, but Chris and his boy, Country had always been best friends. Now with Country being incarcerated, Chris didn't have anyone to talk things over with, so he had to rely on his own instinct and judgment. Even though he was two years older, Quick started out in the same grade with Chris and Country and eventually became a part of their clique. They had been through a lot together, and Chris looked at Quick as one of his brothers.

Quick, on the other hand, only cared about himself. If there was any type of inconvenience with letting Chris stay with him, Quick would have never offered. Chris always gave people the benefit of the doubt, and until somebody crossed him, he treated people like gold. Chris truly believed that Quick was his man. He would need to get back at Manny, but that could wait. If something happened now, all fingers would be pointed in Quick's direction, which would compromise Chris's living arrangement. He dozed off with everything weighing heavy on his mind.

A few hours later, Chris woke up and headed over to Misty's house. They had hooked up right before he got locked up. The two years he spent in GJR was lovely due to her support. Misty used to send letters and pictures, and Chris was the man. Everyone, including the staff, gave Chris his props. Misty was definitely a stunner, half black and half Spanish with olive skin that gave her an exotic look. Getting with her was all by accident. Initially, she intimidated the shit out of him. Misty, without a doubt, was the "baddest bitch" out in the streets. At eighteen, every nigga in the hood had their eyes on her, but Misty shocked everybody when she ended up with Chris.

They had been at the little neighborhood cookout. Chris kept staring and telling Quick how much he wanted her. If it wasn't for Quick calling him a "pussy," he would have never approached her. But Chris was used to proving himself and never backed down from a challenge. So he walked up on her and started a conversation, and ever since, the two had been inseparable. Misty was right by his side during his exile from society. She wrote him every day, and her loyalty made him fall head over heels for her. When he came home, she was there waiting. Now with three months left to graduate high school, Misty was headed to Florida for college. Chris was going with her.

Being on the run enabled Chris to save enough money for relocation. He couldn't go out and floss like an average hustler. On top of that, he was intoxicated by the look and smell of money. He would count it over and over just to touch it. Once he got to Florida, it would be his time to shine.

As he lay with Misty in bed, she could tell something was bothering him. "What's wrong, papi?" she asked, pushing her long, curly, coal-black hair from her face.

"Ain't nothing, mama. Just tired. I can't wait to get out of here," he replied.

The thought of going to Florida with Chris put a smile on her face as she rolled on top of him and brushed her lips against his. The kiss sent a chill through Chris's spine. She pulled away from him slowly, her hazel eyes looking directly into his troubled eyes.

"I love you, papi. Please tell me what's wrong."

Chris trusted Misty more than he trusted anyone. He began to explain what had transpired between Quick and Manny. He also let her know he planned on making Manny pay for his transgressions.

"Maybe you should talk to him," she said.

"For what?" he asked.

"To make sure what Quick says is true."

"My man don't got no motherfuckin' reason to lie to me." Chris grew irritated.

Misty snapped to attention at Chris's tone of voice. She jumped out of bed and looked down at him. "Whoa Papi! You need to watch how you talk to me. I didn't do nothing to you."

"What the fuck you mean! Sittin' here disrespectin' my man. Don't forget he put a motherfuckin' roof over my head when them people wanted to keep me locked away."

"I know what the fuck he did. I also know he was trying to get some of this pussy while you were away. Kept asking why I'm sittin' around waitin' for 'that white boy' as he put it."

Chris was known to play with them guns. This was why everyone talked that "white boy" shit behind his back and not to his face.

Both of their tempers rose.

"Bitch, you done?"

"Bitch! Who you callin' a bitch? Make me call Jesus, motherfucker!" she threatened.

At the mention of Jesus, Chris realized their argument was getting out of hand. He couldn't care less about drama. However, Jesus was his bread and butter. Through Misty, Chris was introduced to her cousin, Jesus—his cocaine connection that most seventeen year olds didn't even know existed. He quickly went from being broke to having money to do what he pleased. Not wanting to argue any more, Chris grabbed his hoodie off the back of the bedroom door and made his way out of her house.

"You fucking puta!" Misty screamed as tears blurred her vision and rolled down her cheeks. She loved Chris, but hated Quick. He was a snake, and she never told Chris about his transgression because one, it didn't work. And two, she knew Chris would end up back in trouble. All she wanted to do was get out of McKeesport with Chris. Now here they were falling out about Quick.

When she first met Chris, he swept her off her feet. He wasn't like anyone else she had been with. Chris was always himself. He didn't try to impress anyone, and he treated her with respect. This had been the first time in all their time together that he had ever raised his voice and called her out of her name.

THE DEVIL'S GAME

All the guys in the neighborhood used to talk shit behind Chris's back trying to get Misty to get with them, but Misty was not interested. She had a man who didn't cheat or hit her, and was a good natured person. She was smart enough to know that all the other guys wanted was sex, and she wasn't going for it. She truly believed that Chris loved her, and one day he would leave the streets. Even though he hadn't graduated high school, Chris was extremely intelligent and could do whatever he wanted to in life. Until that time came, she would stand beside her man and support him no matter what. She wouldn't sit by quietly while he ruined their plans by running to aid Quick, who didn't give a flying fuck about Chris. If Quick was Chris's man he wouldn't have ever tried to get with her.

CHAPTER 4

McKeesport, Pennsylvania was a small city of about thirty thousand people, a hard town that had at one time been thriving with industries. That was until the steel mills closed. When the mills left, so did everything else. Jobs were replaced with hustles and habits. The streets that were once alive with businesses were now littered with drug dealers and fiends, pimps and hoes. You had to be strong to grow up in the "Killa McKee" or anywhere in the Mon-Valley for that matter.

Chris had been introduced to the game at an early age. A product of a single mother who worked two jobs trying to provide for him, and many times leaving Chris at home unsupervised. At the time they lived in one of the worst housing projects in the city plagued with crime, Crawford Village. With no father to look up to, Chris looked up to all the pimps and hustlers. He wanted to be just like them. He used to see all the old heads with their exotic cars parked on Walnut Avenue and dreamed about owning one. As a child, he stood in the mirror picturing himself in furs and gators. Chris used to laugh to himself because he knew deep down inside what he was going to be.

Early on, he learned that he was going to have to fight for his respect in the predominantly black neighborhood, because being a "white boy" made Chris a target. This attributed to Chris's do or die attitude. In his mind, letting any transgression slide would promote weakness, and then people would try him. At thirteen he possessed his first gun when he found it in a car that he had stolen. Sometimes he used to walk down to a secluded part of the river and practice shooting for hours. The feeling he got when he pulled the trigger was euphoric. He knew one day he would experience the feeling again.

Now, as he walked down Pirl Street on his way to a little neighborhood chill spot called the Blue Note bar in search of Manny, he tried to justify his intentions. *This pussy needs to learn a lesson. Me or mines ain't the ones to fuck with.*

The bar was packed and people were pouring out of the door every few minutes trying to get some fresh air. Chris didn't see Manny's car, but he was from Crawford Village just like Chris, so eventually he would be through. On Friday night the Blue Note was one of the spots to be.

As Chris waited in the shadows by the Lucky Spot store, he stared in envy at the people enjoying themselves, coming and going as they pleased. Chris hated being on the run. Now, after the argument with Misty, he began to dwell on her words. Would Quick really try to holler at his girl? If so, was Chris now making a mistake? Why would Manny try to rob Quick if his mother was there? It just didn't make sense, but Chris was having trouble not believing Quick. He wanted to give Quick the benefit of the doubt. But what if he was lying? He turned to walk away when he heard a loud sound system coming down the hill. The headlights brightened the street and Chris recognized Manny's Buick Grand National.

The car was impeccable. Midnight blue with Chrome 100 spoke Dayton wire wheels. Surprisingly, the car turned into the Lucky Spot and parked five-feet away from Chris. Manny got out, and the first thing Chris noticed was the thick Gucci link chain draped around his neck. It was all Chris needed to confirm Quick's story. Instantly, any doubt left Chris's mind, and he approached his target. Stepping out of the darkness, Chris said," What's good, Man-Man?"

Spooked by Chris's sudden appearance, Manny flinched a bit, but then Manny finally recognized him. "Chris, what's going on, baby boy? When did you get home?"

In response, Chris lifted the 9-millimeter Beretta and fired. "You can keep my shit, pussy."

Boom!

People hit the ground at the sound of gunfire and some ran for cover.

The bullet tore through Manny's chest and he wobbled on his feet, wearing a look of surprise that instantly turned into one of anguish. Manny clutched his chest on instinct. His whole upper body must have felt as if it had burst into flames. Without hesitation, Chris fled the scene leaving Manny on the ground fighting to breathe. His last memory was of Chris's dark hoodie as he ran away from the scene. The stars in the night sky disappeared and Manny fell into a state of unconsciousness.

Those who were bold enough to look saw a figure in a black hooded sweatshirt running across the street, and before they could get a good look, he was gone. Then everybody focused on Manny.

"Somebody call an ambulance!" shouted a young woman.

"Yo dawg, that's Manny!" another person said.

A few people ran to his aid. He was still breathing, but the rise and fall of his chest was barely noticeable. Five minutes passed before the ambulance arrived. Manny was immediately loaded up and taken to McKeesport High School where a life flight helicopter was just beginning its descent toward the football field. It transported Manny to one of the major hospitals in Pittsburgh.

Still unconscious, he was losing a lot of blood. The paramedics gave him oxygen and put pressure on his wound. As soon as the helicopter took off he was given an IV.

"I don't know if he can hold on. Hang in there, buddy," said the young paramedic.

The surgeons at Mercy hospital were waiting. Manny was in surgery less than thirty minutes after being shot. The bullet went straight through and amazingly missed his heart by an inch. The doctors became optimistic, and after the surgery all they could do was wait.

Sometime later, he was transferred to ICU where his condition was monitored closely. His mother was the only one permitted in his room and she spent the night sobbing uncontrollably and praying for God to spare her only child. Around 2 p.m. the next day, her prayers were answered when Manny squeezed her finger. She stood and hollered for the nurse. Manny couldn't speak. Tubes filled both his nose and dry mouth. He felt like he was dreaming.

Allegheny County homicide detective, Yuengling waited outside his room. As the nurses came in to tend to Manny, they asked his mother to step outside. When she did, the detective rose to introduce himself, but she cut him off. "They call him Quick. That's who did this to my baby."

The detective knew how upsetting it must be for a mother to watch her son fight for his life. He didn't want to burden her with questions, but his job required it.

"Ma'am, I know this is hard right now, but I need to ask you some questions." Manny's mother just looked at the detective and nodded.

"This Quick, do you know his real name?"

"I can't remember. I think it may be Deon, but I can't be sure."

"And why do you think this boy is responsible for your son's shooting?"

"I caught the two of them fighting on my porch."

"About what?"

"How the hell should I know? Why are you sitting here asking me all these questions when you should be out arresting the person responsible for shooting my son?"

"One more question. What does Deon look like?"

"He's a good-looking kid. Athletic build, medium height. Looks like the R&B singer, Tyrese. I'm sure the police in McKeesport will know him. They know all them kids."

The detective knew he had pushed enough for now. Hopefully, it wouldn't become his problem. He hated to see young people dying over nothing. "Thank you for everything, ma'am. I'll do what I can to make sure your son's shooter is apprehended and punished. Take care."

Manny's mother turned and walked away. She wasn't optimistic. The police didn't care whether Manny lived or died. What happened to her son was to them another opportunity to get a young black man off the street.

The detective didn't even have a chance to explain that he was only there to check on Manny's status. If Manny just happened to die, the case would then fall on his desk. He made it a routine to stay on top of things and not allow things to land on top of him without any preparation. Detective Yuengling

THE DEVIL'S GAME

left the hospital and headed to McKeesport, so he could share the information he had just obtained with the police there.

CHAPTER 5

Manny was dead. Chris was sure of it. He cut through the yards and back alleyways until he crossed Versailles Avenue and left the immediate proximity of the crime. However, he still wasn't safe. He had to get rid of the weapon and get his belongings from Quick. There would be questions, and Quick might be a suspect.

Chris sought revenge on Manny out of pure emotion. Not to mention the sloppy way in which he handled the situation. His argument with Misty had him thinking unclearly. Now as his adrenaline subsided and his thoughts became lucid, he had the sinking feeling that he messed up. Was Quick really the snake Misty claimed him to be? Was there more to the robbery than what Quick had told him? Manny wasn't known as a stickup kid. He was a hustler. Manny had pulled up so quick that Chris didn't have a chance to talk himself out of it. Seeing the chain around Manny's neck set Chris off.

He proceeded to Quick's door cautiously. It seemed safe. Once inside, he realized that Quick wasn't home. Chris ran to his room, emptied the contents of his safe and drawers into two gym bags, turned off the lights and left. He would call Quick later and figure things out. All Chris cared about now was getting out of sight and staying that way.

While walking to Misty's home, the weight of the firearm in his hooded sweatshirt was nothing compared to the weight Manny's shooting put on his mind. He had to keep his head though, and get rid of the gun as quickly as possible. The last thing Chris needed right now was to get caught with the gun.

The first sewer he came to, he removed the gun and broke it down, wiping away his prints in the process. Then he tossed it into the drain.

It took him another five minutes to get to Misty's house. He tapped on her window, and she immediately ran to the front door to let him in.

When she answered the door, he could tell she was crying. "Why Papi? Why did you do it?"

"Do what?" he asked, becoming worried.

"Manny. I heard what happened to him. Lisa just called me. She said Manny just got shot."

"I don't know what you're talking about," he said defensively.

"No estoy stupida, Christopher!" she yelled in fiery rapid Spanish. He stepped in the house and closed the door.

"Everything's all right, mama." Then seeing no reason to continue trying to lie, he stated, "It ain't like anyone knows who did it. The only person who saw me is dead, so fuck it." He shrugged.

"Papi, Manny didn't die." Misty wore a shocked expression on her face. Partly because Chris was so nonchalant, thinking he had killed someone, and another out of concern for the position Chris was now in.

Chris felt lightheaded. Manny's words before he was shot replayed in Chris's head. *"Chris, what's going on, baby boy?"* His chest tightened like a vise around his heart, and it felt like the life was being squeezed out of him.

"How the fuck did he live?"

"I don't know, papi. What are we gonna do?" Misty asked.

What were they going to do? Chris had no idea. He would be eighteen in a month, and he could head to Florida, find an apartment, and lay low until Misty graduated in late June. Then she could join him. He would be running for the rest of his life. The juvenile record would have eventually gone away, but the shooting however, would be tried in adult court. His mother and Misty both begged him to leave the Pittsburgh area and move on with his life. What would his mother say at a time like this? *"Christopher, you can't run forever. Christopher, you really did it this time."*

With nothing left to say, Misty curled up next to her man and cried herself to sleep. Chris only stared into the dark in the direction of the front door, waiting for his time to run out.

While he lay in bed, Chris thought about his childhood and how things had changed so much. He and his best friend Country had always been into mischief, but he couldn't remember when it had gone from innocent childhood trouble to illicit behavior that would earn them incarceration.

At one time, Chris and Country's biggest love was sports. Every year was filled with football, baseball or basketball practice. They would stay on the court or the field practicing until it got dark. But once practice ended, it was back to the gritty reality of the 'hood'.

Not having enough money led to their first petty crime. They each stole a candy bar out of the neighborhood store. Chris remembered not having any money like some of the other poor kids in his neighborhood, and he didn't like watching other kids eat their candy in front of him, so he went to get his own and so did Country. Realizing how easy it was to steal, boosting had become a regular habit for the two young men. Chris was nine years old the first time he got caught. The store's owner never notified the police, opting instead to call Chris's mother. After getting caught, Chris and

Country moved on to something new. They began going through unlocked cars looking for anything of value.

Now as Chris lay in Misty's bed, all of his misdeeds came to mind. Having stolen, sold drugs, hustled, shot and killed, all before becoming an adult. Life didn't seem fair, and as Chris tried to fall asleep, a small tear formed in the corner of his eye. *Why can't I let go of these streets?*

CHAPTER 6

Quick sat in the Elks Club drinking a Hennessy on ice while spitting game to a beautiful, exotic looking female. The woman made every man passing by feel as if it were necessary to stop and chat with Quick just to get a better glimpse of the eye candy by his side. Quick didn't even notice the stares. His mind was focused on Manny's well being. He barely heard a word the woman or anyone around him said.

Quick knew Chris played with them guns. He also knew Chris would seek revenge on Manny, but he didn't think he would try to kill him. He prayed that Manny had seen it coming and realized that Chris was his shooter. If not, Quick would be a prime suspect. Manny's mother saw everything that transpired and would surely lead the police in his direction. From what Quick had heard, witnesses observed Manny pull up and some man walk up to him. Nobody saw who fired the shot. One thing was for sure. If Manny saw him, Chris fucked up letting him live. "Fuck him," Quick said under his breath as he downed his drink. Standing up, he turned to leave and walked right into three police officers.

"What the fuck?" Quick asked, taken by surprise.

"Going somewhere?" asked the black officer everyone referred to as Mister.

"Home, motherfucker!" Quick spat as he tried to walk around the three officers.

The men laughed as Mister turned Quick and slammed him on the bar.

"Deon Smith. You're under arrest. You have the right to remain silent . . . Aw hell, you know the rest." Mister laughed as he led Quick from the Elks Club and into a waiting car.

"What's this all about?" Quick asked.

Talking to his fellow officer, Mister said, "Donnie, when are these assholes gonna learn that they can't run around shooting everyone?"

Donnie shook his head in disgust as they got in the car and drove off.

Before they even put the car in drive, Quick didn't waste a second trying to clear his name. "I didn't shoot nobody. It was that white boy Chris who shot him!" He told the police that Manny had robbed him earlier that day and had taken a gold chain that had belonged to Chris. "The last time I saw Chris, he was carrying a gun. He told me not to worry about it and that he would handle it."

Once they were at the police station, Quick was taken to a cell until an officer finally came and retrieved him. Then another officer led him into an interview room. Upon entering the room, a white man in a suit stood and introduced himself.

"Mr. Smith, my name is Detective Yuengling. You already know Officer Green."

"Mister, you know I ain't do this shit," Quick said to Officer Green.

"I don't know nothin'," Officer Green replied as he walked out and left Quick and the detective alone.

"Listen, Deon," Detective Yuengling said. "Manny Dawkins is in serious condition. This hasn't become my case yet. I'm here so that if that young man dies, my T's are crossed and my I's are dotted. If he does happen to die, you'll spend the rest of your life in prison. So I suggest you don't waste my time and tell me exactly what happened. I'm the only friend you've got right now."

Quick stared ahead, ready to vomit as he thought, *Did Manny tell the police it was me? Why the fuck are they messing with me?* One thing was certain. Quick wasn't doing a year let alone life for Chris. *Nobody will care. Chris is just some white boy. The hood will understand.*

Quick started from the beginning, omitting the fact that he was taking Manny drugs. The way he told it, Manny just up and robbed him for no apparent reason, and in the process took Chris's chain, which he had lent to Quick. It was complete bullshit, but the police didn't care. Chris had eluded them on numerous occasions, and with Quick's testimony, they could put Chris away for a long time.

That night Quick agreed to fully cooperate. He provided them with Misty's address and two signed affidavits. One concerning Manny's role in robbing him, and the other statements Chris had made that implicated him in Manny's shooting.

After being released from the station, the police drove to Quick's home and performed a search of the residence. They determined that if Chris had been there he had packed his things and made a run for it. Their next stop was Misty's home.

At approximately 6:30 a.m., two days after Manny's shooting, a SWAT team silently approached Misty's home. The streets were still quiet that Sunday morning. Chris heard banging on the front door. He climbed out of bed and the front door came crashing down.

"McKeesport police! Search warrant!"

It was inevitable. He was prepared to go to prison. Misty's family would have his back, and Jesus would get him the finest lawyer money could buy. He had $75,000 left after giving Misty $25,000 to help with her move to Florida. Chris also hid some work, so when he was done with his time he would have something to come home to.

Chris was arrested without incident. Handcuffed, read his rights, and then taken to McKeesport police station for questioning. When asked about the shooting, Chris replied, "Eat my dick, pussy."

The arresting officer punched him in the mouth and then charged him with attempted murder, among other things. Chris arrived at the Allegheny County Jail for the first time in his life. As expected, he was being charged as an adult.

When he got there, the officer placed him in a holding cell with four other men. One of the men was a dope fiend, who shit in his pants while going through withdrawal. The smell was unbearable, which eventually led to another man beating the fiend up so the guards would come and place him in a cell by himself.

Once fingerprinted, Chris was sent to another holding cell where he awaited his arraignment, which was held via video. His bail was set at $150,000. Next, Chris arrived in processing, where he was allowed to use a phone while waiting to be taken upstairs.

He called Jesus first. According to the lawyer Jesus hired on Chris's behalf, there was no sense in posting bail since Chris already had a bench warrant from his juvenile case. His lawyer would be down to see him the following day. Chris hung up and dialed Misty. She answered on the second ring.

"Hey, papi," she said.

"Hey, mama. How's my other half?"

"Hurting. I can't believe you're in there. All because of a fucking rat."

"I know, mama. I slipped the fuck up. I figured Manny wasn't gonna keep it in the streets," Chris replied.

"Papi, Manny's talking, but it ain't to the police. They just arrested him for armed robbery. When he gets outta the hospital he'll be down there with you."

"What the fuck you mean he didn't tell? Then who did?"

"Papi, your boy Quick is the rat. He told on you and Manny."

Chris's lips tightened, and his blue eyes turned gray, something that only happened when he was heated. The anger slowly burned through him. He held the phone so tight that his knuckles turned white. "How you know this?" he asked, trying to control his anger.

"Manny's people are telling everyone. They were at the hospital with Manny when he was arrested. Papi, Manny told the police you were his boy and that it wasn't you."

"I can't tell. They just charged me. Did you tell Jesus yet?"

"I was gonna call him. I just heard this myself. The only person saying you shot Manny is your boy." Misty made sure to emphasize 'your boy.' Then she added, "I told you about him."

"Yo, ma, I'm not trying to hear that mess right now!"

"I'm just saying, papi. I love you and try to protect you, but you always gotta be Mr. Gangsta and do it your way."

"Hey Misty . . ."

"Sorry Papi," she said, realizing she was pushing too hard.

They used the last five minutes of their call to discuss their future. Now that Chris knew Manny was keeping it 100% in the street, he assumed he would beat the charge. Of course, he had to do his juvenile time, but that was nothing. Hearing that Quick was telling on him was a totally different issue that Chris was having a hard time dealing with.

Chris walked back to his cell and sat on his bunk as he dissected everything that had happened. The more he reflected on his friendship with Quick, the more he realized that Misty was right. Outside of letting Chris stay at his home, Quick had done nothing for anyone but himself. Anytime he looked out for Chris there was something for him to gain also.

Determined to get even, Chris began to formulate his plan for revenge. When the time came, he was going to make Quick regret ever crossing him. Snitching was unforgivable.

Also, Chris worried about Misty. He knew she loved him, but how much could she take? She had just done two years with him and here he was again, back in jail. The thought of losing her was unbearable. Chris realized he took for granted that she would always be by his side. Now that he was off the streets, he had time to reflect on his way of life and the mistakes he made. At that precise moment, he became determined to use the time in jail to focus on getting his life together. Regardless if he was hustling, he still needed to be a better man and act more responsibly.

CHAPTER 7

Chris had been down in the county for almost two months. He hadn't yet had his preliminary hearing, which had been postponed twice by the prosecutor because Manny refused to testify. They had one more chance. If Manny didn't show up, the charges would be dismissed. Quick's statement meant nothing without Manny's testimony, who like Chris, was also in the county. Manny had been on probation for a gun charge. Therefore, he had a detainer lodged against him.

Chris had yet to run into Manny because of their separation. Because Chris was accused of shooting Manny, they wouldn't likely end up face to face during their incarceration. However, through an old head named Scrappy who got moved to Chris's unit, Manny was able to relay a message to Chris. Manny asked that Chris have Misty call his girl so they could meet up.

Chris was skeptical. He didn't know if Manny would try to get at him by hurting Misty. She would be leaving for Florida soon, and if anything happened to her, Chris would never forgive himself. In the end, he decided to go through with the meeting. After all, Misty hadn't been hiding. If Manny had someone trying to hurt her, it would have happened already.

The meeting between Misty and Manny's girl, Tammy, took place a few days later. The ladies met up, greeted one another, and kept the conversation short and sweet.

"Manny sent me this letter. He told me to give it to you so that you could read it to Chris on your next visit," said Tammy.

Misty took the letter and told her it would be done. With that, the two went their separate ways. Once Tammy was out of sight, Misty opened the letter and read it.

Damn Homeboy,

I see you're playing God now. That shit you did was some snake shit, but I'd let a snake go free in a minute to catch a rat. You know what it is.

"What the fuck is this boy babbling about?" Misty asked aloud as she headed back home.

Misty grew frustrated with Chris's loyalty to the streets. Ever since Chris had been down nobody had sent him a single dime. Yet, Chris would always have her running to the post office mailing money orders to people who were incarcerated. But Chris couldn't even get a letter out of anyone. Misty was tired.

The next morning she woke up and went to visit Chris. She always tried to catch the early visit because there were less people. When she finally got upstairs and saw Chris, she picked up the phone and smiled. "Hey baby."

"Hey mama, how you feeling?" he asked.

"Missing you," she replied without making eye contact. She knew this wasn't the time to gripe.

"So what happened with Manny's girl?" Chris asked.

Misty pulled the letter out of her pants where she had concealed it.

"What the fuck? You on some 'I spy' shit or something?" Chris laughed.

"Shut up, boy! You know they be searching us." She rolled her eyes.

After she read the letter, Chris sat back and dissected Manny's message. After some thought, he concluded that Manny said, "You think it's your job to determine who lives and who dies. Shooting me was sneaky. I didn't see it coming. Go kill Quick and I will continue to keep my mouth shut about who shot me. If I go to jail because of Quick, I will suddenly get my memory back."

So now Chris had to make a choice. Manny was agreeing to keep his mouth shut as long as Chris took care of Quick. *This is beautiful. I was gonna kill that pussy anyway.*

However, the problem was, Chris was still in jail. Even if his charges were dropped, he still had to deal with his juvenile issue. His lawyer assured him that once the charges were dismissed he would be given time served toward his juvenile issue. Then he would be released immediately.

"Get in touch with Tammy. Let her know to tell Manny it's done as soon as I see daylight."

Misty now understood the letter. She had read it a few times before going to sleep the night before. The thought of Chris committing murder left her stomach sour. But if it kept him free and got Quick out of their lives, she would get over it.

There wasn't much to do in the county jail. Chris, who was a Muslim, spent most of his time reading the Quran. He had taken his Shahada, the testimony to Allah that Muslims make, when he was fifteen. An old head named Yah Yah who looked out for Chris was Muslim and was always speaking of Islam. Chris had never considered himself Christian and felt uncomfortable with certain aspects of Christian beliefs. Islam, however, made sense to him, and he accepted it as his faith. A lot of times while in the dunya (world), men of all faiths were enticed by their lower desires. Chris was no different, having fallen from the folds of Islam while running the streets getting money. During his juvenile bid, he had really buckled down and tried to stay within the guidelines set forth in the Quran and Hadith, but as soon as he returned home, he fell back into his old ways. Knowing how out of touch he was with Allah worried him, so he tried to strengthen the rope between him and his creator. He didn't want to hustle forever. Chris knew he couldn't just walk away though. Immediate changes in his life had to be made. He took too much for granted, mainly his own life.

Running the streets could take its toll on the body, so Chris dedicated a few hours of his day to working out. Jesus stayed on him. Having done five years himself, he always told Chris, "If the time comes where you have to go to prison, do the time. Never let the time do you."

Chris made it a point to utilize the time to his advantage. He realized that all the material things in the world could be replaced. However, time could not. For once time is spent it's gone forever.

There was nothing to be gained from playing cards or watching television. Chris told himself time and time again, "I'll leave here a better man."

Finally, his time came. Six months had passed since Chris's arrested. Even though Manny didn't show up at the preliminary, the magistrate still sent the case downtown to big court. It wasn't until Chris's lawyer filed discovery motions that the district attorney finally withdrew his case. The charges stemming from Manny were withdrawn, but the Commonwealth preserved their right to re-file the charges. As promised, the court closed out his juvenile case and Chris was a free man.

When Chris walked out the door, Jesus greeted him from inside his white SL600 Benz convertible. Jesus jumped out the car and embraced his young soldier, "Como esta. Damn boy, you're all cut up."

"Bien," Chris answered, "Didn't have much to do in there but work out, read, and eat."

"Good to have you back, lil cousin. I know mi prima can't wait to see you. I got her a ticket. She'll be here Friday evening."

Misty was now in Florida completing her first semester of college, so Chris insisted that she not miss any classes on his account. Plus, Chris needed some time to get things back in order. Quick was at the top of that list. Manny was still stuck in jail. They offered him two and a half to five years and Quick's punk ass was really testifying.

"Hey, Jesus. Thank you for everything. You made this shit easy," Chris said.

"No problem. Always remember, Chris, a person will be coerced into telling a lot easier if you turn your back on them. That's why I take care of my own. That's what men do."

Chris listened to Jesus, whom he had learned more from than anyone. Chris's father was obsolete. He hadn't heard from him in years. His mother was a great woman, however, she had to make a choice—stay home with her son and starve, or go to work. So Chris learned how to be a man in the streets. Having Jesus as a mentor changed his life. He had values, morals, and discipline most kids his age didn't understand.

"So what's going on with your buddy Quick? I found out where he is staying like you asked," Jesus said.

Chris began to fill Jesus in on his plans. After Chris finished, Jesus looked over at Chris and smiled, "Tu eres el diablo (You are the devil)." Then he asked, "Do you mind if I tag along?"

Jesus loved Chris like a little brother. He saw himself in Chris and he wanted to look after him. He knew that he couldn't talk Chris out of the murder, and honestly he didn't want to. Quick was a piece of shit. But, Jesus would ride along and make sure nothing went wrong since he also had a vested interest in Chris. Chris was one of Jesus's top moneymakers, and Jesus was going to make sure it remained that way.

Not only did Chris not mind, he insisted. The plan involved three people that Chris could trust. He trusted Jesus with his life. The problem was the third person had to be a woman. The only woman he trusted was Misty, and there was no way Chris would allow her to get caught up in his bullshit. Now that Jesus offered his assistance, he would have more resources available to carry out his plan.

Growing up in a neighborhood plagued with gangs and violence, Chris was known to play with them guns. He had found himself in the middle of numerous gun battles, but had only committed one murder. Nobody knew about it.

The man's name was Daniel, one of his mother's boyfriends. One night a few months before Chris went to GJR juvenile home, his mother was thrown through the windshield during a car accident. The ambulance rushed her to the hospital. She was busted up pretty bad. Chris learned that Daniel had been drinking and fled the scene, leaving his mother bleeding on a back road. She sat there for almost two hours before a car finally passed by and went for help. Another hour and his mother would have bled to death.

Chris waited a few weeks and paid Daniel a late night visit. The door was unlocked. When he went inside, he found his target shoveling cocaine up his nose while sitting on the couch watching porn. Chris didn't even notify Daniel that he was in the room. He walked up behind him, placed the gun to the back of his head, and pulled the trigger.

Chris imagined that killing someone would be hard to deal with, but he was wrong. After the murder, Chris went home and made something to eat and called Misty. The first few days after the murder he was nervous, but the police never knocked on his door. Then Chris realized that getting away with murder was easier than stealing a car. Ever since Daniel's murder, Chris had the attitude that he could control whether somebody lived or died. So he was excited at the chance to get back at Quick.

CHAPTER 8

Quick moved to the West End of Pittsburgh to an area known as Greentree Village. It was low key and far enough from the hood that he didn't have to concern himself with running into anyone from McKeesport. The issue with Chris made Quick an outcast. His new spot was a perfect fit, and it was right next to his new chill spot called the Ugly Dog. Here, Quick was able to establish some clientele that allowed him to continue his drug trade. Although the money he generated was nowhere near the kind of money he made with Chris, it was enough to allow him to live comfortably.

Quick became too relaxed too soon and loved his apartment on the 1800 block of Chessland Street. He thought he was straight as long as Chris and Manny stayed locked away. Therefore, he didn't view either one of them as a threat. But time moved faster than he realized while he was starting over and trying to make a name for himself. Being out of touch with the hood, Quick never realized that Chris was out.

Chris was in fact free and had one thing on his mind. Killing Quick. Jesus had a hook up with a chick at the DMV, and for a small fee of $2,500, he was able to get Quick's new address.

Chris and Jesus sat in a black Suburban watching Quick's apartment building, waiting for a sign of their prey. From their angle, they were sure to see Quick. It only took a few hours before they watched him walk out of his front door and get into his red Escort. "Damn, is this dude ever gonna get rid of that piece of shit?" Chris laughed.

Jesus laughed and said, "That pussy won't be buying anything ever again unless we mess up."

Chris tripped off the fact that he was actually waiting to kill somebody. Not just anybody, but his brother from another mother. Things had changed. He had changed. At one time he would be so nervous before committing a crime, let alone killing somebody, that he would have the shits. Now here he sat as cool as a fan. Like they say, "Things get better with age."

Quick turned his car around and headed to the bottom of Chessland Street. He made the left onto Poplar Street, which was where Chris and Jesus were parked. As Quick passed his angels of death, he never noticed the black truck or the two predators waiting to seal his fate. Once Quick reached the bottom of the hill, Jesus started the Suburban, made a three point turn, and pursued him. They already knew Quick spent most of his day at the Ugly Dog, so it was safe to assume he would be headed there now. Their assumptions were correct. As they made the right at the bottom of Poplar Street and onto Noblestown Road, Quick was in the process of parking his ride. Jesus pulled the truck into the plaza's parking lot across the street. Chris was sure of it. Today Quick would pay.

Damn, Quick thought when he walked in the door of the Ugly Dog. A stunning looking Caucasian female with copper skin sat at the corner of the bar playing the Mega Touch machine.

Quick took a seat on the other side of the bar where he had a view of the woman. She stood about 5'4" and weighed about 135 pounds. Her light blue eyes hypnotized Quick. The woman, whose name was Val, was breathtaking. She dressed sexy yet conservative, in a nice pair of blue slacks, white blouse, and black patent leather pumps. Val had the look of a banker who had just left the office. Quick was so captivated by her beauty that he didn't hear the bartender ask him what he wanted.

"Boy, do you hear me talking to you? Get your mind out the gutter and tell me what you want," the bartender named Christina said.

"Damn, my bad. Let me get a Henny on the rocks," Quick replied without taking his eyes off the woman. "Yo Chris, who is that?" he asked Christina as he nodded in the newcomer's direction.

"How the fuck should I know?" she replied, getting jealous.

Even though she and Quick had only slept together once, she really liked him. The sex was amazing. He had been the first black guy she had ever been with, and he was extremely aggressive, which turned her on. He actually liked her too, but there were too many females for him to choose from at the Ugly Dog. He wouldn't ruin it by being locked down by her.

"Yo, send her a drink," Quick said, nodding toward the beautiful woman.

Christina slammed his Hennessy in front of him as she walked over to the woman and said, "He wants to buy you a drink."

The woman sensed the hostility. In response, she smiled at Christina and said, "I'll take a buttery nipple, but only if he comes and does a shot with me."

"What's in it?" Christina asked, clenching her teeth and tapping her fingers on the bar, trying to contain her anger.

"Butterscotch schnapps and Bailey's Irish cream."

Christina stormed away and delivered the message to Quick, making sure that she gave him a piece of her mind in the process.

Quick dismissed her tantrum and turned his attention back to the woman at the bar. He tried not to appear anxious, and nonchalantly made his way over to her. For the first time in his life, a woman intimidated him. Immediately, he was stricken by her beauty, but he tried to not let it show. "Hey Miss Lady. My name's Deon. What you drinkin'?"

"Val," she said and held out her hand. "Nice to meet you, Deon."

Quick gently shook it.

"I'm drinking a buttery nipple. You ever had one?"

"Nah, I ain't never had one of those, but I wouldn't mind trying one some time. You from around here?"

"Just moved down here from New York. It was the only choice I had in order to get out of a bad relationship. But I'm looking for a new start."

Quick nodded that he understood. "So what do you do here for work?"

"Well, my uncle is a tax attorney and he offered me a job as his secretary, so I took him up on the offer. The only thing I left back in New York was an asshole, so I have no regrets. Hell, I'm single, no kids, and right now I'm looking for Mr. Right."

"I guess you came to the right place then," Quick said.

Over the next hour, the drinks were pouring and their words became more sexual. Quick was sure he was going to be inside her by the end of the night. However, Quick was surprised when she asked, "My place or yours?"

"Damn, you get right to the point!"

"Baby, I don't got time to play. I haven't been fucked in over two months."

Quick paid his bill in a hurry, and the two of them headed out the door. Before they left, Quick turned and blew Christina a kiss.

"Drop dead," she replied and threw her middle finger up, seething with anger.

Quick chuckled as he held the door open for Val. As they walked outside, he realized that he had had a little too much to drink. The parking lot started spinning. He didn't even see the black Chevrolet Suburban pull into the lot. He also didn't realize that Val had slipped a Rohypnol pill into his drink.

"Hey, baby girl. You better drive. I'm twisted," Quick said.

"Ahh, the little baby can't handle his liquor," she joked. Then she said, "Come on, honey. My truck is right over here."

He could barely stand up as he staggered after her. He placed his arm around her shoulders as she helped him into the truck. It wasn't until he heard a familiar voice that he realized he had fucked up.

"What's going on, baby boy? I've been looking all over for you," Chris said, looking over the front seat and into the back where Quick sat looking stunned.

Quick knew he was in trouble, but he could barely focus. The last thing he heard before blacking out was Chris's voice. "I'm gonna take my time killing you, motherfucker."

Before pulling out of the lot, Jesus got out the truck and hugged Val. He gave her a long passionate kiss and then thanked her for doing a great job. When he got back in the truck, Chris looked at him with wide, crazy eyes.

"Que pasa?" Jesus asked trying to hold back his laughter after seeing Chris's expression. "I told you I knew the perfect woman whom I could trust with my life."

"I feel you. I just didn't know you were talking about your wife. You could have told me that." Chris laughed.

"Never let your right hand know what the left is doing. She's the only woman I could ever trust, Chris. Sometimes it's good to have a few surprises every now and then. Now the fun begins," said Jesus as they pulled away from the bar and drove Quick away to his death.

The house was located in a small rural community outside of Pittsburgh called Bentleyville. Jesus was in the process of rebuilding it, and it would eventually become his home. It sat on fifteen acres of land, and his closest neighbor was a mile down the road. It was about forty-five minutes south of the city, but this is what made Jesus want it the most. He wasn't the type of man to make enemies. However, he felt safer being tucked away in the country where nobody could find him unless he wanted them to.

Quick had slept all night strapped to a table, and Chris didn't intend on bothering him until he was completely alert. The more aware Quick was, the better. Around 8 a.m., Chris looked up and saw Quick waking.

The first thing Quick realized when he woke up was that he was somewhere foreign. He lay spread eagle on top of a table covered with plastic in the middle of a room. The smell of fresh paint and sawdust invaded his nose. His arms and legs were tied tightly to each table leg. He tried to struggle, but to no avail. Quick knew he was going to die.

He could barely speak as his eyes met with Chris's eyes. His mouth lacked moisture, and a huge lump sat in his throat.

Hung over and fearful, Quick's words were barely audible. "Chris, what's-what's going on?"

"You tell me, Quick. You're smart. I'm sure you can answer that shit yourself," Chris said.

"Chris, please don't do this," Quick cried. "They made me tell. They were gonna put me in prison."

"So you gave them me." Chris let out a cynical laugh. Then his voice rose in anger. "You were like a brother to me! I loved you like my blood. Do you understand that, or are you too selfish to comprehend that? I shot Manny for you, motherfucker! Then on top of everything, you lied. Not to mention you tried to get at my bitch!" Chris paused as his eyes became glossy. His emotions were overflowing. The internal conflict of love and hate only fueled his anger. Finally he spoke. "So now, I'm gonna kill you. I'm gonna make you suffer. You won't leave this world until you experience the same pain you caused me."

Without another word, Chris bent over and retrieved a drill from the floor. As he stood, he squeezed the trigger. The motor screamed forebodingly and so did Quick.

"Please. Please, don't do this!"

His pleas were ignored. Chris placed the bit on Quick's knee. The drill dug into Quick's flesh. He screamed out as skin and bone were torn apart. Quick's wrists and ankles were bloody from trying to escape the shackles and torment. Relentless, Chris removed the bit and drove it ferociously into Quick's other knee.

"How does that feel, motherfucker? You fuckin' rat! Don't start crying now, bitch. You wasn't crying when you was snitchin'. So take this shit like a man!" Chris shouted.

Consumed with emotion, Quick's screams only fueled Chris's desire to administer more pain. He moved from

Quick's knees and began drilling into his shins. Quick's screams became agonizing groans. Tears rolled down his face and onto the table.

"Please don't do this," Quick begged.

Chris showed no mercy as he reached in his pocket and retrieved a utility knife. Quick's eyes widened in terror as he shook his head.

"You like to run your mouth? I bet you won't use these lips to tell on anyone ever again," he said.

Chris held Quick's head firmly against the table and plunged the blade under Quick's bottom lip and sliced through his face. He repeated the same act across his upper lip. There was no attempt at precision. Chris savagely removed Quick's lips from his face. When he was done, ragged flesh dangled from the gaping hole. Blood poured from his wound, and Chris suddenly began to feel nauseous. His anger began to simmer, and he realized he was out of control. *I'm trippin'*, he thought. But still he wasn't done. He removed the last prop from the floor and placed it on Quick's chest. Quick yelled out in anguish as the hot iron sizzled. Smoke rose into the air as the clothes iron seared his flesh. Finally, his body shut down, and he blacked out from the pain.

Chris stood over Quick and watched the hot device eat away at his victim's chest. Finally, he walked outside to join Jesus on the porch. As he left, he looked back over his shoulder and said, "Play with fire you get burned, motherfucker!"

Jesus sat on the porch eating McDonalds.

"You want one?" Jesus asked, trying to hand Chris a breakfast sandwich.

"How the fuck can you eat right now?" Chris asked, pushing his hand away.

"I didn't kill him. Besides, have you ever run over an animal with your car?" "Yeah, I hit a raccoon once. What the fuck does that got to do with anything?"

"Did you miss dinner that night because of it?"

"That's different. It was an animal. We're talking about a human being."

"No. That's where you're wrong, my friend. We're dealing with a rat. Now go make sure he's dead so we can clean up and get out of here."

Chris turned and walked back in the house. The smell of burning flesh filled Chris's lungs. It wasn't repulsive. It actually smelled like someone had been cooking.

When he reached Quick, he noticed the iron burning away his flesh a little at a time, yet he was still breathing. In response, Chris removed the pistol from his waistband, pointed it at Quick's head, and pulled the trigger. Quick had suffered enough.

He unplugged the iron to let it cool as he threw all the other evidence into a garbage bag. Once the iron cooled, he did the same with it. With Jesus's help, Chris rolled Quick up in the plastic tarp that had been placed underneath him to catch any blood that fell. They tied up the tarp with a rope, and the two men carried the corpse outside to the fire pit.

The fire had already been started. Quick's body was tossed in the fire and Jesus dumped a bucket of thick liquid on Quick. Flames rose and danced in the air. The fire rose over fifteen-feet high.

"What the fuck was that?" asked Chris.

"Homemade napalm. Mixed some Tide with some gasoline and you got some mean shit," Jesus said proudly.

"Where the fuck you be learning this shit?" Chris asked.

"I got this crazy ass white boy that taught me all that shit. Even gave me a book called, *How to Blow Things Up.*" Jesus laughed.

The two stayed around until the fire burned out. They didn't take any chances and scraped together what remained of Quick and shoveled it into a small metal box. That, along with all the other evidence was tossed in the Monongahela River on the way home. Quick would never be seen again.

Chris should have felt some remorse. Regardless of Quick's transgressions, the two had been friends for the majority of their lives. Chris however, felt none. Quick had violated a major rule of the game. Everything Quick had done in the dark had come to light, and Chris realized they had never really been friends. In Chris's mind, the murder was justified and necessary. He quickly put it out of his mind and focused on the road ahead. With Quick out of the way, it was time to get money, and that's just what Chris planned on doing.

As for Quick, Chris wasn't worried about his murder. Quick had been in hiding, and as long as they never found a body he would be presumed missing. It wasn't like the police would be knocking down doors to find a piece of shit that tried to play both sides of the fence.

CHAPTER 9

Hey papi," said Misty as she ran to Chris and threw her arms around him. I missed you so much," she said, kissing him softly on the lips.

"I missed you too, mama," Chris said as he threw her suitcase in the trunk.

"Whose car is this? It's nice as hell."

It's mine, mama. Jesus got it for me. He said it was my welcome home present.

The day after Chris took care of Quick, he and Jesus were riding around when Chris let him know he wanted to go look at some cars. Not only did Jesus take him to look, but he also bought him the car.

Chris liked fast cars. He picked out a 1986 Pontiac Grand Prix with the 305-v8 engine. It was in pristine condition. Chris drove off the lot and straight to Audioworx on Route 51 where his man Lonnie dressed it up with wheels and a system. Now that he was free, he could spend some of the money he had given Misty to hold before he went to jail.

"So I guess we're driving back to Florida," said Misty.

Chris knew it was coming. Ever since he got released, all she spoke about was him coming back to Florida with her. He didn't know how he was going to break the news to her, but he chose to wait until later on that night.

"So where you want to eat?" he asked.

"Anywhere, as long as it's with you," she responded.

Her response planted a deep-seated guilt inside Chris. His choice not to return to Florida was going to crush her.

The rest of the drive was filled with stories of college. She hated this professor but loved this course. Blah, blah, blah.

They chose to eat at Olive Garden. Chris ordered the chicken alfredo, and Misty ordered the lasagna. They sipped iced tea and nibbled on breadsticks while they waited for their order. Out of nowhere Misty looked at Chris and said, "You're not coming back with me, huh?"

Caught off guard, Chris began to stutter. He tried to speak, but only a sigh came forth as he lowered his head, ashamed to be letting her down.

"Papi, don't do this to me. We had plans. You promised."

"Mama, I'm still coming. But I can't just up and leave right now. Jesus needs me."

"Fuck Jesus. Jesus ain't the one you're fucking, Christopher!" she said, raising her voice. People began to stare.

"Whoa, mama. Watch ya mouth," Chris warned. Then he added, "I love you, but me and Jesus got business. Once that business is through, I'll be there. I can't just walk away. I need to get this money."

"Forget the money, papi. I can get money off my dad. He'll give us whatever we need."

"Stop playin' with me. That's his money. I don't take nothin' that I ain't earned. I can get my own," Chris said.

"Am I not worth it? Is Jesus, the money, and the streets more important than me? I'm tired of being second all the time," she cried.

"Don't get it twisted. In my heart you're always first. I gotta get this paper though. Life ain't free, Misty. I'm sorry, but my father ain't paid like yours."

"That's not fair. It's not my fault my father got money. You're acting like there is something wrong with it." Tears began running down Misty's face. She quickly wiped them away.

"I'm sorry. You're right, mama. Let's just drop it for now. We'll speak about it later," Chris said, eager to change the subject.

The rest of the meal was silent. They asked for some to-go boxes and made their way to the car. Chris walked to the passenger side and opened the door. As Misty started to get in the car she stopped and said, "I won't leave you. If you don't come to Florida then I'm moving back here."

Chris grabbed her firmly by her shoulders and pulled her toward him so they were face to face. "Mama, I can't let you do that. You've been talking about going to Florida since I met you."

"Christopher, unlike you, I put us first. I believe in us, and if I have to go to school in Pittsburgh, then oh well. I will never choose anything over you."

A bullet in the head would have been less painful. Chris realized at that point just how special Misty was. He didn't deserve her. Now instead of being a man and following her to Florida like he had promised, he was going to allow her to throw away her dream and follow him into the gutter. To chase his street dreams.

He couldn't ask for a better woman than Misty. He didn't want her to leave Florida. She had been determined to go there as long as they had known one another. But there was a part of him willing to let her drop out and come home to fill the void her absence left in his life. Chris was ashamed at the thoughts, but that didn't deter him from his decision. If Misty came home that would be her decision. Chris would make sure that she was always taken care of.

CHAPTER 10

A few months passed. It was New Years 1996. The chauffeur opened the door to the cocaine-white stretch Lincoln as Misty climbed inside. She wore a white Versace dress and a mink shawl that set Chris back $2,500. Chris's view of her hourglass figure from behind made him realize that the money was worth it. Her arm and leg muscles were toned from her daily workouts, and her stomach was solid like concrete. Chris could picture her nude body under that dress and the smell of her Dior perfume. The image aroused him, but he fought back his desire.

Chris wore a black Armani suit and a pair of David Eden Croc's. His jewelry was modest, no flashy chains, just a Rolex Submariner on his wrist that Jesus had given him as a gift. He was always worried about drawing attention to himself. However, Misty was another story. Diamonds accentuated every part of her body with the exception of her ring finger. People couldn't help but stare at the attractive couple as they entered the fine dining establishment.

Dinner with Jesus and Val at the Tin Angel on Mount Washington was amazing. A small dish of fruit was followed by a huge tray of meat, cheese, and vegetables. Misty and Chris both had chicken marsala. Dessert was New York style cheesecake followed by a delicious chunk of pineapple marinated in a mint liqueur. Moet flowed all night. Neither Chris nor Misty were old enough to drink. However, Jesus was a regular and the servers weren't going to mess up their tip making a big deal over some alcohol.

The remarkable view from their table prominently displayed Pittsburgh's beautiful skyline outside the large windows. The tourists would ride the inclines to the top just to take pictures. Chris couldn't have set up his proposal in any better place. It was perfect. Misty had proven herself to Chris since the first day they met. Ever since being home from jail he hadn't been with another woman. He only wanted Misty, and he was determined to seal the deal. Everybody's attention was focused on the view, so when Chris took a knee it went unnoticed. When Misty turned, she almost fainted. She clutched her chest as if her heart stopped.

"Yes! Yes!" she screamed, almost knocking Chris over when she hugged him.

The patrons in the restaurant realized what was happening and stood to clap. Chris looked at Misty and said, "This ain't no engagement ring. It's a friendship ring."

The ring was immaculate. A flawless five-karat with a triple band sheer radiance green amethyst. The pave setting made the diamonds shine brilliantly.

Playfully, she started to choke him as he laughed. Then he got serious and looked into her eyes. "I know we're young. I know that at times I'm a knucklehead, but I love you. Your good balances out all my bad. Without you I'm incomplete, and I want to make sure we're together forever."

Misty and Val both had tears in their eyes.

Jesus started talking shit. "Mi prima got you whipped."

Chris gave him the "fuck you" look. To make up for his remark, Jesus bought a bottle of champagne for every table.

THE DEVIL'S GAME

They left the restaurant around 10 p.m., already twisted. They decided to go back to Jesus's home in Bentleyville. All the remodeling was complete and there was plenty of room for both couples. Chris tipped the limo driver and they got in the car with Jesus and Val.

The couples watched the ball drop from the comfort of the game room. An hour later, Jesus and Val left Chris and Misty alone and they turned in for the night. Chris led Misty to the deck and motioned her toward the Jacuzzi.

"Boy, are you crazy? It's freezing out here," she said.

Ignoring her complaints, Chris removed the cover. Set on making love to her in the hot tub, earlier he had turned on the heater so the water would be hot by the time they came out. Misty let go of her argument as Chris began to remove her clothes. Goose bumps spread across her body as her nipples hardened. He led her into the water, removed his own clothes, and then joined her. At first they were playful, splashing and wrestling like kids. On cue, Chris pulled her close and kissed her passionately. He felt her breasts against his chest, which caused his erection to grow. He pulled her closer while she grinded her pussy against his long shaft. Even being completely submerged in water he could feel her juices, and he longed to be inside her. He pursued her, but she grabbed his hands and pinned them down. She continued to tease him. Suddenly, she released her hold and turned her back on him as if she was going to get out of the hot tub.

"You gotta taste what you wanna fuck, papi," she said. Misty placed her hands on the edge of the Jacuzzi and lifted her ass out of the water. He immediately slid behind her and spread her ass wide open, sliding his tongue deep inside her. She bit her arm to control her screams. She tried to get free, but Chris held her around her waist and wouldn't let go.

"Papi, please. I, I, I can't take it. Papi, I'm cumming!" she screamed.

Finally, he released her as she dropped lifelessly into the water.

"Give me a second," she pleaded as he tried to pursue her.

Chris looked at her hungrily. "Okay, I gave you a second." He smirked.

He wasn't going to be denied and he pulled her toward him. She sat on his lap and placed her head against his shoulder. He put his finger under her chin and lifted her head to kiss her neck. Then Chris placed her nipple in his mouth and gently massaged it with his tongue.

"Mmm papi," she moaned. Her hormones began to race again. She straddled him, and this time she didn't tease. Reaching down and grabbing his hard dick, she placed it inside her. His toes instantly curled, and he fought the urge to climax. He tried to think of everything but sex, so he could prolong the ecstasy. It just did not work. She threw her hips back and forth rocking on her pelvis. He lasted five minutes. The orgasm started in his stomach. The hot liquid coursed through him as it erupted from his manhood and was deposited deep inside her. He moaned and scratched her back like a bitch. She kissed his ear, and he pushed her away as she laughed.

"What's wrong, papi? Ain't no fun when the rabbit got the gun."

He realized he had been exposed and laughed about it. At that moment he knew there wasn't going to be an extended engagement. He was going to lock her down as soon as possible. A woman like Misty came along once in a lifetime and she belonged to him.

THE DEVIL'S GAME

After Chris and Jesus had talked her into finishing the semester at school, that winter, Misty had just moved back from Florida. She transferred her credits to California University of Pennsylvania. Chris had purchased a log home in Monongahela, a medial point between McKeesport and the University. It was a small, but comfortable place. They had some land and very few neighbors and behind their home was a trout stream. Chris had a pavilion built, so they could host cookouts for the family without having to worry about the weather. They had a horseshoe pit, volleyball net, and a swimming pool installed. He spared no expense and bought everything brand new. He even bought two ATV's so that he and Jesus could ride. There were miles of woods behind the home, and the two men could spend all day riding. Chris was excited to finally make it out of the hood. He could relax at his new home and not have to worry about stick up kids, the police, or catching a stray bullet. He loved McKeesport, but the peace and tranquility his new environment provided were priceless.

Money was rolling. After Misty went back to school, Chris dived into the drug game headfirst. Now that he could move about freely, he was going through five kilos a week, which netted him a weekly profit of $10,000. He didn't deal with many people. His best friend, Country had just come home from juvenile. Like Chris, he was loyal and mature beyond his years. However, unlike Chris, Country did the time he was given instead of being on the run. Country, unlike Quick, could be trusted with Chris's life. The two men were inseparable. There were moments when people thought they were going to kill each other, and they wouldn't speak for days. Then one or the other would call, and it would be as if nothing ever happened.

Now that Country was back on the streets and ready to hustle, Chris started him off with a half kilo. Chris was getting the whole kilo for $22,500, so he gave Country the half for $12,500. After awhile the half kilo wasn't enough, and he was meeting Country every two days. To eliminate the constant rendezvous, he tossed Country two kilos a week and charged him $50,000.

Chris's other major customer was surprisingly Manny. He came home shortly after Quick's murder. The first meeting between the two provided some insight. Quick's murder was never mentioned. When Chris learned the underlying facts of the robbery, he apologized profusely over and over until Manny finally told him to shut up.

"I'm still standing. That shit's in the past," said Manny.

Chris didn't completely believe Manny would forget that easy, but he still fronted him a kilo. He felt guilty for his actions. There was a chance that Manny would fuck him out of spite, but Chris would take that chance. Now, just like Country, Manny was going through two kilos a week. Naturally, Chris kept his guard up, but he was slowly accepting the fact that Manny forgave him.

The last kilo out of every pack Chris kept for himself. He broke it down into eighth and quarter kilos. He could have made more money breaking it down to ounces, but the less people he dealt with, the better chance he had of not getting jammed up by the police.

As the money stacked and time went on, Chris was constantly paranoid. The Grand Prix he bought was too flashy and now stayed in the garage most of the time. He bought a brand new Nissan Maxima and left it just the way it was. Better to play it safe than getting caught up by the po-pos.

CHAPTER 11

The wedding was held on June 15. Only immediate family and close friends were invited. Jesus's property had a small lake that set a beautiful scene for the affair. He had a gazebo built which would serve as the stage for the special occasion. The setting was perfect. After their vows were exchanged and they were united as one, everybody retreated to the reception being held at The King of the Hill restaurant.

Misty's father, Rico gave an eloquent, heartfelt speech inside the classic, medieval Shakespearean themed restaurant. He had been honored to give Chris his daughter's hand in marriage. In private, Rico told Chris that he felt safe that Chris would protect her and be an ample provider. He knew what Chris did for a living. Initially, Rico had funded Jesus's operation. The two had been partners for years. However, Rico made the decision to go legit and open a construction company. He prayed that eventually, Chris would do the same and walk away from the streets and do something positive with his life.

Soon dinner was being served. The food was delectable and the mood was festive. Misty and Chris were leaving for their honeymoon early the next morning, so they left the festivities around 11 p.m. They made love in the limousine all the way to the hotel at Pittsburgh International Airport.

Early the next morning, they boarded their flight to Cancun, Mexico. The honeymoon was a gift from Jesus and Val.

When they landed, it was as if they were in another world all together. The airport sat in the middle of a jungle. The air was thick and humid. By the time they reached customs, their shirts were soaked in sweat. Another hour passed before they finally walked out of the airport and to their awaiting car.

They arrived at the Camino Reale. The hotel sat at the tip of the peninsula, and its beauty mesmerized them. It had three restaurants, a pool, and lagoon. The floors in the bedroom were marble. Their back door sat less than fifty feet away from the Caribbean ocean. As the waves crashed onto the rocky shore, they felt the spray of the water as they sat on the patio and sipped their drinks.

They spent their time shopping and taking in the sights rather than waste it in the clubs. They took the popular Jungle Tour. A small jet boat was provided as they made a voyage from the Caribbean ocean, through a lagoon, and to the Atlantic Ocean. There, the couple snorkeled at the reefs. The water was so clear you could see a mile under water.

Misty's favorite attraction was the flea markets. She had bought so much stuff that they had to have it sent home. Her focus was the beautiful tapestry and other knick knacks. Chris purchased a chessboard and pieces that had been carved from stone. They were both amazed at the bargains for merchandise that reflected hard work and astounding skill.

Chris could never remember being so at peace, but it was all ruined when four days into their honeymoon there was an urgent message to call home. The message turned out to be from Misty's parents, Beverly and Rico. Misty and Chris both prayed that her parents were okay.

THE DEVIL'S GAME

When Misty called, her mother answered on the first ring and after the initial formalities, her mother broke the news. "The Feds got Jesus and Val."

"For what? Are they looking for my husband?" Misty asked nervously.

Chris snapped to attention while Misty's mother explained everything.

As soon as they hung up, Chris was on her. "What's that all about?" he asked.

"Jesus and Val got pulled over on the highway. That's all my mother knows. Apparently, it's pretty bad. Their arraignment is tomorrow."

"Where did they get knocked?"

"Somewhere out by Harrisburg,"

Chris wanted to vomit. Jesus was his bread and butter. If something happened to Jesus, Chris would be on his own. Although Chris's lifestyle was humble compared to the average hustler, he still had larger spending habits than normal. He managed to save about $150,000 and had about $100,000 in flip money. *How long will that last?* he wondered.

Like so many hustlers, Chris wasn't prepared beyond the game. He lived for the moment, never taking into consideration what he would do without the game.

"Call the airport. Get us on the next flight home," Chris instructed.

Misty didn't argue. She called the travel agent back home instead of the airport. The earliest flight was the next day, and they would get in during the evening hours.

They spent their last night at the hotel bar where Chris drowned himself in Tequila.

The following morning, Chris was nursing a hangover while the couple packed to leave.

"You okay, papi?" Misty asked.

"Yeah, I'm cool," Chris replied without any conviction.

"You sure don't seem okay. I know you're upset, but Jesus is in jail, not you."

"What the fuck does that mean? What? I'm supposed to be happy about this shit?" Chris asked fiercely.

"Maybe instead of acting like it's the end of the world, you should be appreciating your freedom and your wife. It's always Jesus this and Jesus that. Quit worrying about Jesus and worry about yourself."

"Get the fuck out of here with that mess. I wouldn't be shit without your cousin. Without him I'd still be a fucking petty ass car thief," he said angrily.

"Or maybe you'd be in college doing something with your life. Jesus only cares so much about you because you make him money. But me, papi, I was there when you didn't have shit."

Chris knew she was right. It pissed him off more as he threw on his shirt and left. He wasn't trying to hear her mouth right now. He had just turned nineteen years old. All he knew how to do was hustle. Jesus was the closest thing he had to a father, and now he was in jail.

He returned to the room with only enough time to grab his bags and leave. They were halfway home before a word was spoken, but the guilt from their argument was tearing Chris apart.

"I'm sorry, baby girl. I'm just a little fucked up about all this. It's our honeymoon, and we should be celebrating." She took Chris's hand and laid her head against him. She hated the thought of losing Chris to the game. If only she could convince him to do something with his life without offending him. If she pressured him to go legit he might feel as if he wasn't good enough. That was the last thing she wanted to do.

They landed back in Pittsburgh on time and were met by Misty's father, Rico, who explained that a random traffic stop got Val and Jesus caught up. In Chris's mind nothing just happened at random. Rico's narration of his conversation with Jesus led Chris to believe they had been set up. Jesus had told Misty's father that the police kept searching as if they knew he was dirty. Jesus said that during the search they found a wire tucked under the carpet in the rear of the Suburban. They followed the wire to what looked like a battery terminal. Further search provided them with a second terminal. They pulled a cruiser to the rear of the truck and ran jumper cables from the cruiser to the terminals and almost shit themselves when the whole floor lifted and exposed twenty-five kilos of cocaine.

At the arraignment earlier that day in front of a U.S. Magistrate, Jesus was denied bail. Val's bond was set at $250,000.

"I'll call the bondsman when we get home," Chris said.

"It's already posted. Her father took care of it," Rico replied and then added, "They're up there waiting for her to be released now."

It wasn't until the next day that Val finally called Chris and let him know she was all right. She also let him know that Jesus was okay and that whenever Chris had a chance she needed to sit down and go over some things with him.

"I'm on my way now," he told her.

The house in Bentleyville was about twenty minutes from Chris and Misty's home. He made it there in ten minutes. Val saw him coming down the drive and waited for him at the door. They sat at the kitchen table. She brought two beers out the fridge and handed one to Chris.

"Somebody set us up, Chris," Val said.

"I was thinking the same thing, but who knew yinz were going? Not only that, who knew there was a stash spot that had the police searching so heavy?" Chris asked.

"A few people knew there was probably a spot. Jesus let all his guys know so they could get them installed. But only one person knew Jesus was going to cop."

"Who?" asked Chris.

Val took a deep breath and exhaled. "Rico."

Chris almost threw up. "You mean Misty's dad, Rico?"

"He's crooked as hell, Chris. Why do you think he is so comfortable with your business? How do you think he got his business? He just knows how to cover his tracks, which is why you never knew."

Chris never thought about it. He assumed Misty's dad was just cool and he understood. Rico was always at work, running a large construction company and doing well for himself. In a million years he couldn't picture "Pops" pushing work.

"So you think he told? Why would he? What would he gain by telling on Jesus?" Chris asked Val.

"I don't know. Maybe he got caught up in something and is trying to save his own ass. All I know is it came out of Jesus's mouth first," she replied. Then she added, "Chris, Rico has got to go."

"Val, is you trippin'? That's Misty's dad. My father-in-law. What the fuck I look like killing him?"

"If he's tellin' on Jesus, it's only a matter of time before he tells on me or you and that can't happen. Jesus was his nephew for Christ's sake. His blood!" Val said angrily.

Val had a point and Chris knew it. It was tearing him up inside. "How can I face my wife if I slump her dad?" Chris asked more to himself than Val. He wanted to talk to Jesus about it, but when he had a chance to talk to Jesus on the phone, Jesus wouldn't say a word. He just kept saying, "Don't worry about it, my friend. I'll be all right."

"You can face her as a free man or a convict. The ball's in your court," Val said, giving a slight shrug.

"I'll take care of it. I don't want to, but I will. You made your point," Chris said remorsefully.

Chris changed the subject. "So you gonna be all right on money? I got a few bucks put aside, but without a connect I'm fucked."

"Baby," Val said as she pinched Chris's cheek. "You didn't lose no connect. I put Jesus on. My family is Jesus's connect."

Chris just put his head down on the table and laughed. "Are there any other bombs you want to drop on me before I leave?"

"Nope. Just take care of Rico, and you're the man now. You are the man." Val pointed at Chris.

CHAPTER 12

The full moon illuminated the night. Chris pulled the Nissan Maxima to a stop a few blocks from the Elks Club in McKeesport and walked through the back alley toward the establishment. Deep down he wished Rico's truck hadn't been there, but it was. Killing Quick was easy. Quick had crossed him and there was absolute proof. *What if Rico is innocent?* Chris thought. However, he couldn't take that chance. Chris had to eliminate any threats. His instinct to preserve self was in high gear and there was no turning back.

He found cover in some bushes with a clear view of Rico's truck. Now all he had to do was wait. Rico was a creature of habit. At almost 11 p.m., Chris knew his prey would be leaving soon. Rico appeared at approximately 11:26 p.m.

At the sound of footsteps, Chris jerked to attention and quietly got to his feet. Moving quickly out of the bushes, Chris quickened his pace to head Rico off at his vehicle. Startled, Rico looked up and saw Chris. "Boy, you scared the shit out of me. What the hell you trying to do? Give me a heart attack?"

"I wish it was that easy," Chris replied as he lifted the pistol and pulled the trigger.

Rico never had a chance as the bullet entered his forehead and blew his thoughts out the back of his head. Chris stood there and looked over the dead man with shame in his eyes.

THE DEVIL'S GAME

The sound of people heading toward the gunshot to investigate sent Chris into a run until he was safely at his car.

He started his car and drove quickly to the Tenth Ward section of McKeesport. He pulled his car down the boat ramp that served as an entry point to the Youghiogheny River. He broke down his weapon and tossed it into the dark water, and then got into his car and left.

The thought of facing Misty worried Chris. He wasn't a great actor, and he never lied to her. When his pager went off and he saw the number for home, he dreaded the thought of returning her call. It had to be done. He retrieved his phone and dialed home. She answered immediately.

"Chris, come home!" Misty cried out.

"Baby, what's wrong?" Chris asked, trying to sound concerned and surprised by her emotions.

"Somebody—somebody just shot my daddy," Misty said, sobbing.

"What! Who shot him? What are you talking about?" Chris asked.

"I don't know. Just please come home."

"I'm on my way, baby girl. I'll be there in twenty minutes."

"Hurry," she begged.

Chris heard a dial tone. His stomach turned, and he forced the bile back down his throat. His loyalty to the streets would now haunt him forever. Misty would never believe that her father was in any way connected to Jesus's business, let alone snitch on him.

If Misty found out that he killed her father, she would flip the switch on the electric chair herself. *How can I love this woman and hurt her so bad?* Chris thought. The guilt was unbearable as he prepared to face his wife.

When he got home, he found Misty curled up on the couch in a fetal position clutching a pillow. She could barely lift her head to see him enter the room. He hurried toward her and knelt by her side, pulling her to his chest.

"Why my daddy? He never hurt nobody," she cried.

"I don't know, baby," Chris replied. "People do things we may never understand." Chris was surprised how easily he fell into the role of comforter. His guilt subsided some as he held and consoled his wife. They lay on the couch for a little while longer before Chris forced her to get up so they could go be with Misty's mother, Beverly.

When they arrived at her house, Chris noticed Jesus's Benz parked in the driveway. *That's one bold bitch*, Chris thought. Then he realized he was equally shady for his role and dismissed the ill feeling.

Misty's mom appeared to be holding up surprisingly well. Val was sitting with her, and he could tell that both women had been crying. Beverly had just come from identifying Rico's body. It seemed her main focus was the arrangements. Her husband had only been dead a few hours. Chris conceded that, that was Beverly's way of dealing with it.

She told Misty as much as she knew. People heard the gunshot, but nobody saw a thing. Rico still had his wallet, so they didn't think robbery was a motive. Chris and Misty were both shocked when her mother blurted out, "It was probably over some hussy he was fucking."

Chris's jaw dropped. Misty started screaming when her mom looked at her and coldly said, "Your father wasn't what you think. You're gonna find out sooner or later, and I'd rather be the one to tell you. You're father had more women in his life than I care to mention."

"It sure didn't stop you from being in his house and spending his money," Misty spat.

"You can be mad at me, but don't get it messed up, young lady. I loved your father and I love you. I didn't leave because of you. After you left for college, I started sleeping in your bedroom. I'm too got-damn old to be starting over," her mother said.

"Let's go," Misty said to Chris as she got up and stormed out of the house. Chris got up to leave and Val rose to walk him to the door. They were in the foyer when Val leaned in close and whispered in his ear. "You handled your business well, Christopher. Now it's my turn to deliver. I'm gonna make you a rich man."

It was more than a whisper. The way Val's lips brushed against his ear was erotic. He felt his manhood twitch. *What the fuck was that all about?* Chris thought, uncomfortable with his own reaction to Val. Jesus was his man, and he would never cross him. *Why the fuck was she all up on me like that?*

CHAPTER 13

Three months had passed since the wedding, Jesus's arrest, and Rico's death. Val promised that Chris would be the man and she kept her word. With her help, Chris was running through about fifteen kilos a week, and as far as he could tell they weren't in any danger of running out of drugs any time soon.

The prices allowed Chris to give his people love. Val charged him $18,000 a kilo. Her people gave them to her for $17,000. She was the one who made the trips and took the risks on the highway, so Chris was more than happy to agree to her terms. With the prices he was paying, he sold the kilos for $22,500. Even with a loss here and there, he made over $60,000 per week.

Chris made it a point to put a grand a week aside for Jesus. Jesus had entered into a plea agreement, and the U.S. Attorney had agreed to drop all charges against Val. He was looking at a minimum of ten years. The lawyers were waiting for his pre-sentence investigation report to come back before they could know for sure. Chris hated seeing his man in there, but that was the game. Taking the hit so that his wife could walk said a lot for Jesus's character.

Chris wasn't so sure about Val's loyalty to Jesus though. She had been getting carried away with the flirting, and it made Chris uncomfortable. He didn't cheat on Misty. He looked down on dudes who preyed on another man's girl. The problem was, Val was so damn fine he was having a hard time keeping her out of his mind.

With Val supplying his work in abundance, the streets now belonged to Chris. Other dudes were doing their own thing, but not like him. He still tried to keep a low profile and dealt with very few people. Manny and Country were still loyal. Val had hooked him up with one of Jesus's boys from Donora named Benny. The three men moved the majority of Chris's weight. It kept him out the streets and under the radar. *I'm untouchable,* Chris thought as he pulled into the rear of a small bar where he hung out at in Monongahela called Hitches Hut.

A mixed crowd filled the small establishment and the chicken wings were off the hook. The bartender, Trent, was his man, so he used the spot to meet Country, Manny, and Benny. Monongahela was the perfect city to conduct business. It only had a population of about ten thousand people and two police patrolling the street at a time. As long as you didn't do anything to draw attention to yourself they would not bother you.

Country sat at the bar waiting when Chris walked in. "Damn boy, your five minutes is an hour."

"Whatever," Chris replied. "You waited, didn't you?"

The two men laughed as they embraced and sat down to have some drinks.

"How many you bring me?" Country asked.

"Five. They're in my ride."

"Cool. I brought $125,000. That covers the last pack plus twelve-five on this one, so we'll be at a hundred even."

Chris did some quick math in his head and replied, "That's what's up."

Business was out of the way. The two men relaxed for a minute and enjoyed their meal. When they finished, Chris walked Country outside to make the exchange. They were almost at Chris's car when the door to a blue minivan in the parking lot beside Chris's car slid open. Chris and Country were taken by surprise.

"You know what it is," said the masked man as he jumped out of the van and put his pistol to Chris's head. The driver jumped out and held a twelve gauge on Country.

"Nah. You tell me, pussy? What is it?" Country spat.

"It's my pay day or your funeral. Your choice," said the man with the gauge.

Country was a big brother at 6'5" and weighing 280 pounds. He didn't scare too easily, and this time was no different. He answered the ultimatum with a right cross to the man's chin thinking the man was bluffing. The man stumbled but pulled the trigger. The blast threw Country against Chris's Maxima.

The man holding the gun on Chris turned toward Country and Chris took off for cover. He almost made it to the corner when he heard the sound of gunfire. Chris yelled out in pain as the slug tore through his shoulder. The impact knocked him off balance and sent him to the ground as he crawled, struggling to reach cover. He made it around the corner, grabbed the gun from his waist, and returned fire. His mind was consumed with the vision of Country's body going limp. He had to get to his man. The Glock .40 spit lead at the men as they jumped in their van and fled. There was nothing more Chris could do as the van sped off down the street.

Chris ran to Country. He was still breathing. Chris heard the sirens, but there was no escape. Within minutes, they arrived at the scene.

"Get on the ground! Drop the gun! I'll blow your fucking head off!" was repeated several times.

Both men were transported to Mon-Valley hospital and then airlifted by a Life-Flight helicopter to Allegheny General. Neither of the men's wounds were life threatening. Had the robber not loaded the shotgun with birdshot, Country would have been dead. Chris lost some blood and had some muscle damage, but would be back to normal in a few weeks.

Country was released from the hospital the next day. Chris was also released, but was subsequently arrested for possession of an unlicensed firearm, reckless endangerment, and discharging a firearm within city limits. His bail was set at $25,000, and he posted it on the spot.

The lawyers promised to keep Chris out of jail, but he was going to have to plead guilty somewhere down the road. Chris hated the thought of pleading guilty, but he would have no choice. His biggest concern now was finding out who tried to rob him.

Chris decided to lay low for a few weeks. He took Misty to Hidden Valley Resort. They had been there a few times before, and they always had a good time. It was a very laid-back place where people could relax. The beginning of October was a little chilly, so they spent most of their time in the room relaxing. A lot of things had happened since being pulled away from their honeymoon. They needed the time to reconnect. Misty was going in one direction trying to do things that were positive. Chris was running full speed ahead in the opposite direction.

"I wish our life was always this peaceful," Misty said.

"Yeah, this is nice," Chris replied.

"Then why do you keep doing it, Chris? I'm not trying to get on your back. The last thing I want to do is fight. But I'm scared of losing you. Seriously, papi, when is it enough?"

"I really don't know, baby girl. It's more than the money. People depend on me. I told myself once if I made a million I'd walk away. Thing is, I'm damn near there and I'm setting new goals," Chris said.

Hearing Chris say he almost had a million shocked her. He never talked about his money or the streets anymore. She knew he was making money, but a million dollars . . .

"Do you seriously have that much?" Misty asked.

"Nah, mama. *We* got that much," he said with a smile.

The thought of him having that much money disturbed her. She realized that if a million wasn't enough, then it would never be enough.

"Baby, just be careful. After losing my dad and Jesus going to prison, you're the only man in my life that I can depend on. I need you out here." Then she looked up at him and whispered, "We need you."

"Who's we?" Chris asked, laughing.

"Papi, I'm pregnant."

"What the fuck? Are you serious?" Chris pulled her close and showered her with kisses. He was so excited he didn't know what to say.

"I guess you're happy." Misty giggled.

"When did you find out?" Chris asked. He put his hands on his head and paced back and forth in disbelief.

"When what?"

"When did you find out you were pregnant?"

"The morning you got shot. I was waiting for the right time to tell you," she said. "And when they told me you got shot I didn't know what to think. I didn't know if you were going to even live to see your baby. When the police came to the house, the only thing they told me was you had been shot. They didn't know your condition. Do you know what the drive to the hospital was like for me?"

"I'm sorry, mama." Chris grabbed Misty and pulled her close. His stomach knotted up at the thought of hurting her.

Chris was so caught up in the streets that he never stopped to think of how it affected Misty. Now he was trying to see things through her eyes. He truly was sorry. The more he tried to avoid hurting her, the more she got hurt. *I gotta make some changes,* he thought.

CHAPTER 14

Chris continued to lay low till after his preliminary hearing. Country, Manny, and Benny were handling business and product was still moving. Word finally got back to Chris about the attempted stick up. He could never understand the power of pussy. Dudes would say and do anything to get or keep it. Now that Chris's shoulder was feeling better, he was ready to seek revenge.

"Yo," Chris answered his phone as he was just pulling up to his house.

"Good news, fam'. I came across that info you been looking for," Benny said. "You gone trip when I tell you what the fuck went down."

"I'll see you at Hitches around seven, fam'," Chris replied and hung up.

He called Country and told him to be at Hitches around seven that evening. Ever since the robbery, Chris had been on pins and needles. The fact that he didn't know who tried him was eating him up. He was always looking over his shoulder. Now instead of being the prey, he was the predator. He had a wife and a child on the way. No stick up boy was going to take him away from them.

All three men arrived at Hitches around the same time. They each took a seat in the corner, and once Benny had their undivided attention, he told Chris everything.

"Yo, this shit all started when some young boy named Richey was out with my sister, Jessica. Chris, you had your '86 Grand Prix in the shop and must've been just picking it up. Jessica said the car was looking fresh as hell with orchid paint, white leather interior with orchid piping and shit. She's really into tricked out cars," Benny said.

Chris nodded. "All right. Yeah, I do remember that day. I had the roof chopped off. Me and the dude who did all my customization stood outside the shop in the parking lot while he showed me how to attach the soft top," Chris replied.

"Right. About that time, Richey and Jessica were just riding by." Benny got into the details of the story just as his sister Jessica had told him.

"Oooh shit, did you see that ride? That shit is off the hook," Jessica said.

"Fuck that nigga!" Richey responded.

"Why you always hatin'?" Jessica asked.

"That white boy think he's all that. Fuckin' McKeesport nigga think he can come up here and do his thing. That's why I gave him the business a few weeks ago," he exclaimed, *trying to impress Jessica with his gangster.*

"Boy whatever. Apparently, he ain't worried about your ass 'cause he's still out here in some fly shit while you're still riding in this funky ass Honda," she teased.

"Bitch, who the fuck you think you talkin' to? Just 'cause your brother got a few dollars and these other niggaz is scared, don't think I won't smack the shit out of you," Richey threatened.

"I wish you would." Jessica laughed in his face.

SHAWN 'JIHAD' TRUMP

"Whop!" The sound of the smack echoed throughout the car. Richey back handed her so hard he almost snapped her neck.

"Get out my car, bitch!" He laughed as he pulled to the side of the road.

"Nigga, wait till I tell my brother," Jessica said, slamming his door.

Benny hit his hand against the bar, bringing them all back to the present. "Five minutes later, that was the story she told me from a pay phone. I'm still fucked up about dude having the balls to put his hands on my baby sister."

"What else she say?" Chris asked.

"That Richey said he gave some white boy named Chris the business. Jessica thought y'all was beefing and she asked me if I knew you. I only told her that I heard of you. Then I went to pick her up and knew I had to holla at you ASAP."

"So where this dude lay his head?" Country asked.

Benny gave them Richey's mother's address. "That's where he lives," he told them.

"Cool. We'll take care of it," Chris replied.

"I'm trying to ride with yinz. He smacked the shit out my sista," Benny said.

"You gonna have to sit this one out," Chris said, explaining to Benny that he might be a suspect because of the incident with his sister.

"There ain't no telling who Richey told about the incident with your sister. What I need you to do is take your sister and moms away somewhere. Get one of the condos up Seven Springs and don't leave they side. Come back in a few days, and this shit will be done and over with. Keep all your receipts," Chris said, beginning to orchestrate the whole plan in his head.

Chris was anxious to get Richey out of the way. He still didn't know who Richey's accomplice was, or how he even picked Chris as a target, but he would find out. Until Richey was dead, Chris just wouldn't sleep right.

The next morning, Benny took his family away just like Chris had instructed. Benny didn't know what Chris's plans were, but Jesus had once told him that Chris was "barbaric" when he got mad. So whatever happened to Richey was sure to even the score after what he had done to Benny's sister.

At about 8 p.m., Country picked Chris up. The ride from Chris's house to Donora took about ten minutes. They drove by the address on Twelfth Street. All the lights were on, but they didn't see Richey's car, so they pulled up the street and waited.

Chris and Country had put in work together before, but this was their first time catching a body together.

"You good?" Chris asked.

"You know me. It's whatever," Country replied.

"You know what's crazy, fam'? These dumb motherfuckers are about to die and they didn't even get a dime. They're about to die for nothing."

Country didn't say anything, but he listened to Chris. He didn't try to understand the world or the people in it. He just rolled with whatever wave was sent his way. Chris and Country were completely different people. Chris planned everything. Even though Chris lived for the day, he still planned for tomorrow. Country, on the other hand, just didn't give a fuck.

They sat for almost an hour before Richey finally pulled up. They watched Richey run in the house. Country started the truck and pulled up the street, so that they could get away without the truck being seen. Even though the ride was stolen, they didn't want the police to get a description. The last thing they needed was to get pulled over fleeing a murder scene. They hopped out the truck. Country reached into the backseat and pulled a machete off the floor.

"What the fuck is that for?" Chris asked.

"I call this my 'make a motherfucker talk' knife." Country laughed.

"You got issues." Chris laughed.

They made their way to Richey's house and were walking up the steps when all of a sudden the front door began to open. When Richey saw Chris's face, he tried to slam the door shut but Country was too quick. He lowered his shoulder and threw himself against the door. It flung open, and the force sent Richey sprawling to the floor at his mother's feet. She almost jumped out of her skin at the sight of two men standing in the living room. She tried to speak, but Country smacked her in the mouth and told her, "Shut the fuck up!"

Chris held the captives at gunpoint while Country searched the house for anyone else. Once he finished, they tied their victims up.

"Richey, why are they doing this?" his mother cried.

"I don't know," he answered.

"Oh, he knows. See, ya son like to try and rob people. Ain't that right, Richey?"

Richey wondered, *How the fuck do they know it was me?* "I don't know what y'all talkin' about," Richey said, staring at the two men with wide scared eyes.

"Oh yeah." Country stood over Richey with a pistol in one hand and a machete in the other. "How about I refresh your memory?" Country turned the gun in his hand and brought the butt of the gun crashing down on Richey's shoulder. The cracking sound of Richey's bone made Chris wince and his mother scream.

"You're hurting him!" she said as tears poured from her sorrow-filled eyes.

"I ain't gonna sit here and play games all day. There are two questions, Richey. One. Who put you on us? Two. Who was your partner?" Country asked.

"I told you I don't know!" he screamed.

Nobody, including Chris, saw it coming. Country raised the machete and stepped toward Richey's mother. He brought it across her neck with such force it took her head clean off her body as crimson rain showered the room. He turned to Richey with menace in his eyes and told him, "I swear to god if you don't start talking I'm gonna start cutting you the fuck up."

"Mom!" Richey screamed as he started rocking back and forth. "I swear I'm gonna—"

Country brought the gun crashing down on his other shoulder.

"God! Please stop," Richey begged.

"God? You're crying for God? I'm God, motherfucker!" Country screamed. "You better get to talking before I get to cutting."

Chris stepped in front of Richey, certain that Richey knew he was going to die. His pain was so overwhelming that he began to lose focus. He felt as if the world was spinning as he started going into shock. Chris didn't want that to happen. He needed to know everything.

"Richey. Look at me, Richey," Chris said.

The young man shook as he tried to look Chris in the eyes. Chris spoke softly, hoping that Richey might respond.

"Who was with you that day at Hitches?"

"H-his n-n-name is C-C-Corey. Corey Je-Jefferies," Richey replied.

"And how'd you know about me?" Chris asked. "Who set me up?"

"This white girl named Amy at the bank next door to Hitches. I had just met her. She would be on the phone with me talking about how she could see you doing business right out her window. She saw you and him passing bags back and forth. I knew what it was, so I laid on y'all. She let me know what kinda car you drive and all that mess, so I did my research. I would go meet her for lunch and shit. But look, man, she don't know nothing. I swear," Richey said, now calming down and beginning to beg for mercy. "Please don't kill me."

"I won't, Richey. I promise." Chris laughed and got up and walked off.

Country stepped forward and subjected Richey to the same gruesome decapitation that his mother endured. Then the two men exited the house quietly, so that they didn't draw any unwanted attention. Eventually somebody would find the bodies, but Chris didn't care. He wanted to send a message to Richey's partner, Corey. They hadn't left any evidence that could connect them to the scene. There could only be speculation.

Chris walked back to the car in silence with Country right behind him. When they jumped in the car, Chris finally realized that his victim's blood dotted his clothes and body.

THE DEVIL'S GAME

"How the fuck am I supposed to walk in the house like this? What the fuck am I gonna say to my wife?" Chris asked.

"Tell her we was huntin' snakes," Country said sarcastically.

"From now on, dog, no knives. I officially don't trust you with anything sharp."

"Whatever," Country said as he turned up the music and threw the truck in drive.

Instead of going home, Chris called Val who met him immediately. When he got in her car she hit him with a barrage of questions.

"Is that blood? Whose is it? Are you in trouble? What happened?"

Chris didn't want to talk. "I'll tell you later. Just get us to your crib."

Before going in the house, Chris stripped down to his boxers and gave Val instructions to burn his clothes. She took them and headed to the fire pit.

The November air around him was frigid. He still hosed himself off. The last thing he wanted to do was have traces of blood inside Val's house. After thoroughly rinsing himself, he headed inside for a hot shower.

Chris and Jesus were roughly the same size, so Val brought Chris some clothes and a pair of Timbs. He finished showering and then got dressed and met Val downstairs in the kitchen where she had poured him a drink. Before sitting down, he threw the amber liquid down his throat, grabbed the half-full bottle of Hennessy, and took a seat at the table. Val stared at him a minute before speaking. "You want to talk about it?"

"Caught that pussy who shot me," Chris replied and kept swallowing the liquor.

Val didn't say anything else. Chris wasn't going into details, and she wasn't going to push. Instead she got up and walked toward him. She stood behind him and began to rub his shoulders, hoping to help release some of his tension. He surrendered to her hands. The Henny was starting to affect him. It wasn't until he felt his crotch stiffen that he stood and backed away.

"I don't want to keep you up all night, Val. Plus I know Misty's wonderin' where I'm at."

Val didn't relent as she stepped closer, backing him into the cabinets. As Chris looked down, her nipples showed through her white tank top. He tried to run, but his legs wouldn't move.

"Chris, I'm tired of playin'. I want this dick," she demanded as she started to unbutton his pants.

He tried to push her away, but his attempts were futile. "What about Jesus? And Misty?"

"I'll be almost fifty when Jesus gets home, Chris. And I don't want to marry you. I just wanna fuck." She wrapped her hands completely around his manhood as she tried to pump the life out of him. He melted into her touch. Knowing she had him, she dropped to her knees and slid his dick deep in her mouth. With fluid motions, she slid it in and out squeezing his muscle with her jaws.

"Are you gonna fuck me, baby?" she asked.

She got her answer when he grabbed her by the hair and lifted her off her knees. He forced her to turn around while he ripped her shorts off. Slamming her over the table, he got behind her and placed the head of his dick against her hot pussy.

"Is this what the fuck you want?" he asked as he entered her slowly and pushed as deep as his length would allow.

"Yes. Yes. That's what the fuck I want. Fuck me, Chris. Fuck me!" she screamed.

What started as a slow exotic thrust turned into a savage drilling as he slammed himself deep inside her. Every time he entered her, he felt her juices explode on his legs until he couldn't hold back any longer. His last thrust sent his hot cum deep inside her as he pushed harder so that she would feel every inch. She screamed out in ecstasy as her body began to quake. Neither participant moved. He stayed inside her for minutes, but they seemed like hours. When the sensual feeling began to fade, he finally pulled out as she tried to gather her balance and stand. As she turned to look at him, his guilt was instantaneous. She knew it too. Val bent to grab her shorts and looked up and said, "Quit trippin'. It's just a fuck."

Chris had never cheated on his wife. He didn't have to. She was fine as hell and fucked the shit out of him. She held him down in every possible way. What about Jesus? He wasn't much older than Chris, but Chris looked at him like a father. Jesus taught and gave him everything. He sold out everyone he loved for a piece of ass. Chris was so caught up he didn't realize Val was waiting at the door to take him home.

"Are you coming?" she asked.

Without responding, Chris followed her out the door. The drive home was silent. Chris got out of her car without saying shit and walked toward his house.

"Hey Chris!" shouted Val.

Chris turned toward her. "What's up?"

"Are we cool?" she asked.

"No doubt," he said as he turned and walked into the house. Misty was waiting at the door.

"Why were you with Val? And why the fuck is you wearing something different than when you left?" she asked.

"Not now, Misty," Chris pleaded.

"What you mean not now? And you smelling like a bottle of Henny?" she hollered.

Misty wasn't the insecure type. She trusted Chris completely. Lately, he had been acting different. It was like he was two different people. She didn't know what was going on. He used to tell her everything. Now his life was a secret. She didn't see the change coming. It was gradual. After her father was killed, his attitude shifted. One minute he was one way, the next he was totally opposite.

"Why don't you talk to me anymore? Are you fucking someone?" she asked.

"Hell no! I ain't fuckin' nobody," Chris said. *She must be psychic.* "Why are you trippin'? You want to know what the fuck is wrong? I hate my life. You want to know where I was? I just watched the pussy who shot me get his fucking head chopped off. Is that what you want to hear? I don't tell your ass nothin' 'cause I don't want to pollute the one thing in my life that's pure. I want out of this fucking game but I'm stuck. I don't even got a fucking GED. What kind of job do you want me to work? What you want from me?" Chris hollered as he grabbed his keys and slammed the door behind him.

Misty tried to run after him, but he started his car.

"Chris! Please don't leave!"

She watched him pull out the driveway and disappear into the night. She backed up against the wall and slid down to the floor crying. "I love you, Chris."

CHAPTER 15

Boom! *Boom! Boom!*
"Who the fuck is banging on my door?" Country said as he grabbed his Desert Eagle from beside his bed and went downstairs. His first guess was the police. If it was, then he knew it was serious and he only had a plan A. Take out everyone he can. There was no other option for him. Any case he got would be a serious one that would give him double digits in the joint. He would rather take his chances in the streets than with a judge.

"Who is it?" Country hollered through the door.

"Open up, fam'. It's me," Chris said.

Country opened the door. Chris stood outside with a bottle of Henny in his hand. Country moved aside as Chris staggered through the door.

"What's up, my nig'? You all right?" asked Country.

"Yep, I'm as good as I'm gonna be," Chris slurred.

Country knew something was wrong, but he didn't press the issue. It was 3 a.m. Country had never seen Chris stay out past midnight. Chris took a seat in the chair and Country sat on the couch.

"I fucked up, dog," Chris said. "I fucked up bad."

Country began to worry. Richey had only been gone six hours. He prayed Chris hadn't done something to get them caught? "What's up, fam? What'd you do?"

"I fucked Val." Chris looked down at the floor.

"That's it? If that's fucking up, I wish I was all the way fucked up. That bitch is bad."

"That's easy for you to say. You're not married. And Jesus ain't ya man," Chris replied.

"You act like you ain't ever cheated on Misty," Country replied. "It's fucked up about Jesus, but fam', he is gonna be gone for decades. Not years. *Decades,*" Country emphasized. "They gave that boy 240 months."

"I never have, fam'," Chris said.

"Never what?" Country asked.

"I never cheated on her. Shit, I didn't have to. I know you might think that's crazy. But why should I throw my dick on the chopping block? All these bitches out here burnin' or got that monkey. Not only that. I love the shit out of my wife. How am I gonna throw that away over some pussy?" Chris replied.

Fuck that! Country thought, but kept it to himself. Misty was a bad bitch, but Val was on a whole other level. He had only met her a few times. Every time he saw her, she was on his mind for days. Plus, Country was never settling down. Bitches were too scandalous. He would refer to women as "sperm receptacles."

"Damn dog. Now that you mention it, I never really saw you with another bitch. I don't know how you do it. I do know one thing, if you don't take your ass home she really gonna think you fucking someone."

"You're right, fam'." Chris got up, dapped his man and left.

THE DEVIL'S GAME

Driving home, Chris was feeling better. It was a twenty-five minute ride from Country's house, and Chris began to yawn. His eyelids got heavy. The effects of the alcohol attempted to put him to sleep. While passing Mitchell Power Plant headed into the small borough of New Eagle on State Route 837, Chris began to drift away. A blinding headlight that seemed dangerously close to his vehicle brought him out of his attempted slumber. The sound of metal on metal was deafening, and Chris's car began to tumble until it settled on its roof. It felt like a dream. He heard someone, but could not open his eyes. Then suddenly, the sound dissipated and Chris drifted away. His car looked like it had been scrapped. The passenger side door touched the center console. The roof had trapped Chris inside, requiring him to be cut free. The car that hit him barely appeared damaged. When the firefighter pulled Chris from the car, blood dripped from his face staining everything in his path. Everyone presumed he was dead. Once they realized that he was still breathing, he was rushed to the hospital.

When he awoke, he heard the sound of a heart monitor, a device he became greatly familiar with after his shooting. He knew he was in the hospital, but his room was dark. The only illumination came from the hall and the green line monitoring his life. Misty sat beside his bed. Chris tried to speak, but his mouth was dry. She looked up when she sensed his movements. Hitting the button for the nurses, she rose out of her chair and eased close to her husband.

"Baby, I'm so sorry. I'm so sorry. Please forgive me. I swear I'll never accuse you of anything ever," Misty cried, remembering the scene that brought her to Chris's bedside at the hospital.

Once again the police had shown up at their home and informed Misty that Chris had been rushed to the hospital.

Before they said anything, she broke down crying believing that he was dead. The remorseful look in their eyes was the same one she'd seen a month prior when he had been shot. Chris was her whole world. If something happened to him because of her pushing him away, she would never forgive herself. Her tears became uncontrollable, and she began to get dizzy. Then her feet gave out. The police immediately radioed for a paramedic. When they arrived at the scene, Misty had regained her posture. The police scared her so bad that she fell into a state of shock and became disoriented.

"Is he dead?" she had asked.

"No ma'am, but he is pretty bad," the officer replied.

"What happened?"

"There was a car accident," the officer said and then paused. "Ma'am, alcohol was involved, and we found a gun on the floor. Chris is going to be charged with possessing that firearm unlawfully. He keeps digging himself a hole."

Misty just put her head in her hands and looked at the floor as the paramedic continued to check her out. After he was done, he directed Misty to make an appointment with her doctor to have a checkup.

"Can I see him?" she asked politely.

"Of course, we haven't filed any charges yet. He's in pretty bad shape from what I could tell."

Misty excused the police from her home and followed them. When she made it to the hospital, she was directed to ICU where Chris was being tended to. Most of his wounds turned out to be minor. He was required to get stitches and had a pretty bad concussion, which caused him to go in and out of consciousness, but overall he would be okay. However, all Misty could think about was their argument and the guilt. She somehow felt that this was all her fault.

The nurses began to check on Chris while they waited for the doctor to come in. Misty began to explain to Chris what was going on.

He learned that a drunk driver coincidentally fell asleep at the wheel and flew through the stop sign and slammed into Chris. What were the chances that Chris was also drunk? They found an empty Hennessy bottle in the car. To make matters worse, Chris was strapped.

"They found the gun, papi. They are going to arraign you when you get out the hospital. I left a message for the lawyer," she told him.

Chris just closed his eyes. *I'm already fightin' one case. Now this shit.* If he had just kept his ass home where he belonged he wouldn't be going through this.

In addition to the new charges he was facing, Chris was banged up. A golf ball sized knot sat on the side of his head, and twenty-seven stitches decorated the opposite side. His body felt like a truck hit him instead of his car. He had been in and out of consciousness all day. The doctor diagnosed him with a concussion and scheduled him for more tests. Chris was surprised to learn the accident occurred almost twenty-four hours ago.

The following evening Chris was released. He was to return in seven days to have his stitches removed. He needed to see a neurologist for a checkup. His lawyer had already arranged an arraignment, and Chris was released on $10,000 straight cash bond. He had a preliminary hearing scheduled for the following week. Once again, Chris would be forced to plead guilty. Six months shy of his twentieth birthday, and his record just kept getting worse. Silently, he wondered if he would make it to his twenty-first birthday.

CHAPTER 16

Y o! What's going on, fam'?" Country hollered as he walked into Chris's house.

"Ain't shit," Chris replied as he stood to greet his man.

Two weeks had passed since the accident. Chris had listened to the doctors and gotten some much-needed rest. He was still a little sore and dealing with an occasional headache. Other than that he was fine.

Misty was grateful to have her husband at home. She kept worrying about the baby. Between the shooting, arrests, and Chris's accident, she was a nervous wreck. It would also be the first Christmas since her father's death. Sensing that Chris and Country needed some space, she excused herself.

"Now I see why you don't cheat. Wifey got a fat ass," Country said playfully.

"I'll shoot someone over my broad, dog," Chris replied.

"Nigga, that's why you all cased up now. Keep playin' with them burners acting like you're John Wayne or something," Country joked. Both men shared a laugh. Then they got down to business.

Ever since the night with Val, Chris wanted to avoid her as much as possible. He questioned his willpower. Using his physical condition at the time as his excuse, he doubled his order and paid for the work up front. He owed $270,000 for the fifteen kilos he had gotten on consignment. When Val returned from New York with the thirty kilos, he gave her $540,000. He would be able to avoid her for a couple weeks.

As they made the exchange though, Val was all about business and nothing was said about what had happened between them. She asked him about his new charge and chastised him about messing up over dumb shit.

"You keep bringing all this heat on yourself. You need to grow the fuck up," she told him.

All Chris could do was agree. He knew he was slipping, and he promised her that as soon as he tied up some loose ends he would fall back.

"What kind of loose ends?" she asked.

"The kind that rob people," he answered.

Benny had found out everything he could about Richey's friend, Corey. Country would take care of him. Chris was trying to maintain a low profile. The last thing he needed was another case. Once Corey was gone he would be able to relax. He probably was seeking retribution for Richey's murder. People didn't usually get murdered without reason. Chris intended to send Corey a message with Richey's murder, and if Corey was any kind of friend he would be trying to pay Chris back.

A few days passed before the murder scene was discovered. A neighbor called the police when she had gone over to visit and walked in on Richey and his mother's bodies. The horrific murder ran on KDKA for three days and still there were no suspects, but Corey would know.

They decided to give Richey's girl from the bank a pass. She had witnessed what she believed to be a drug deal and told Richey not knowing he would try and rob Chris. They chalked her up as a dumb bitch who didn't know how to mind her own business. There was a chance that Richey could be lying about her limited involvement, but seeing your mother's head get chopped off had a way of bringing out the honesty in a person. They also determined that killing Richey wouldn't set off an extensive investigation. Killing a white woman who worked at a bank would set off an all-out war against crime.

Getting Corey was turning out to be harder than Country anticipated. After Richey's murder, he was shook. He seemed to have disappeared. All Country could do was wait for him to show his face. Until then, business was handled with caution. Chris kept his face out of the streets, and Country dealt with Manny and Benny. The more separated Chris became with the streets, the more he considered getting out of the game completely. Now that he had a kid on the way, things were different.

Chris wanted to be there for his child. His dad had never done shit for him, and he was determined to not follow in his father's footsteps. Walking away from the streets wasn't a simple matter though. The game was always calling him. It wasn't just the money; it was the power, notoriety, and feeling of success. He was a young kid from the projects. Because of him, he and his boys had money to do what they wanted. Everyone looked up to him because they believed he had made something of himself. Having a nice home, car, and wife made him feel successful. Growing up without anything would often leave a person feeling insecure. Chris would speak about himself with arrogance, as if his shit didn't stink. The truth was, Chris needed to be looked upon as successful. He loved the fact that people noticed him and liked him. It fed his ego and made him feel important. He was a hood star.

Chris promised himself he would get out the game. Week in and week out he broke that promise. "Why get out? Country does all the work. The only people I deal with are Country and

Val. The chances of the police getting me are close to none," he had explained to Misty over and over again.

The months began to roll by, and Misty was starting to show. Their relationship had improved. Chris did all his running around while she was in class. When she was home, so was he. Chris was becoming extremely protective of both her and their child. It annoyed her at times, but she was enormously grateful to have him there. Plus, it was kind of cute to see her "gangsta" husband cooking, cleaning, and pampering her.

Tonight he wasn't doing any cooking and cleaning. It was May 25, 1998, and Chris was celebrating his twentieth birthday. Misty had made reservations at Ruth Chris Steakhouse. From there they were going to the Double Tree Hotel. She took his phone off him. There would be no distractions during their night out. "I want you all to myself," she said.

Chris didn't have any problem with it. He had heard about pregnant pussy from Benny. "Man, that shit is so motherfuckin' hot and wet," Benny had told him.

Benny was right on point. On top of her pussy feeling like heaven, she always wanted to fuck. Chris was always ready to accommodate her.

They rode down to the city in Chris's brand new silver LS 400 Lexus. It was his birthday present to himself. Misty's mother was kind enough to put it in her name. She loved Chris like her own son. After Rico's death, Beverly was left a substantial amount of money. Chris silently wondered if Misty's mother was a happier woman with Rico gone.

Traffic heading toward downtown Pittsburgh was atrocious. It was bumper to bumper and Misty wanted to play.

"Hey papi," she whispered seductively. "You know you've never made love to me in a car. I have this fantasy . . ."

"What kinda fantasy?" Chris asked as his dick jumped knowing where she was going with this.

"That we're stuck in traffic and my pussy is screaming for you, so I start stroking you like this." She unbuttoned his slacks, pulled his throbbing dick out of his boxers, and began to stroke it. He was so hard the veins in his dick looked like they were going to explode. She rubbed his shaft as she took the head in her mouth and teased it with her tongue.

"Holy shit! You're gonna make us crash," Chris said as the car jerked forward.

Misty's mouth felt so good Chris had to brace himself. He saw traffic in front of him inching forward, but he was scared to take his foot off the brake.

"Baby, you gotta let me drive," he pleaded.

"You don't like it, papi? You want me to stop?" she teased.

Hell no he didn't want her to stop. He hit his turn signal and made a right off Route 51 and parked in an alley behind A-1 Auto Mart. He quickly threw the car in park and put his seat back.

"Oh yeah, papi," she said as she sucked him off.

He watched his manhood disappear between her full lips.

"I wanna fuck you so bad," said Chris.

She released him from her mouth and said, "Anything you want, baby."

She moved the passenger seat back and turned so she was facing him. From the windshield her ass was visible as it stuck out from under her dress.

This bitch don't got no panties on. When did she start walking around without panties? Chris thought. It turned him on even more as he climbed over the console. They didn't have much room to work with. Chris slid his tongue inside her pussy. She hugged the reclined seat. Her knuckles turned white from squeezing the fine leather so firmly.

"Chris. Oh my God. Papi. Stop. I'm, I'm, oh God. I'm cumming!" she screamed as her juices flowed into Chris's mouth. He needed to be inside her. He rose and began to enter her.

"Papi, please, give me a second. Papi, please."

Chris wasn't going to be denied. Her pussy was so sensitive. She couldn't hold her balance as she collapsed onto the seat. Chris was relentless. The sound of his dick slamming into her wet pussy made him push harder and deeper. Her body lay flat on the seat and Chris was hitting it from behind. His whole dick was massaging her spot. She came so hard that her body quaked and she bit the seat. The head of Chris's dick expanded as he dumped his hot liquid deep inside her.

Chris knew he had gotten the best of her. Being a smart ass, he quickly slid his dick out of her. She was so sensitive that she almost fainted. She screamed out, "I know you didn't!"

Chris laughed as he opened the car door and slid out, so he could adjust his clothes. She tried to move, but her body was too weak.

"You okay?" He laughed.

Her hair was matted to the side of her face with sweat.

"I'm good. I just hope you didn't put any dents in our baby's head."

"Yo, that ain't funny," he replied.

Chris was so caught up in the moment he had temporarily forgot about the baby. She saw his worried expression.

"It's okay, papi. Quit worrying."

"I wish it was that easy. That's all I do is worry. I'll probably be bald in two years from stress," he joked.

"I can deal with you being bald. Just don't go losing no teeth on me." She laughed.

Chris returned to the driver's seat. Traffic was beginning to ease up. They made it to dinner and ate quickly. The only thing on Chris's mind was getting Misty to the hotel. The sexual escapade in the car had his sex drive in full gear. During dinner, Chris couldn't take his eyes off Misty. The five years they had been together was like a dream to him. All of a sudden reality hit him, and he realized just how lucky he really was. The weight she was gaining from the baby only made her more beautiful. She had an angelic glow. God had chosen her to be a vessel for his seed. He silently prayed he would never be without her. He had to get out of the game. The thought of dying or going to prison never scared Chris. However, the thought of being without Misty terrified him. She completed him.

CHAPTER 17

The day after Chris's birthday, he and Misty checked out of the hotel around 9 a.m. While unlocking the house door, Misty heard the phone ringing. By the time she got inside, the ringing stopped. It immediately started ringing again. She grabbed it on the first ring.

"Hello."

"Misty, where's Chris?" Manny asked, sounding upset.

"What's up, Man-Man? You all right?" she asked.

"Yo, I need to talk to Chris. Please tell me he's there."

"Hold on, Mann. He's about to come through the door." She waited to pass the phone to Chris. When he took the phone she said, "It's Manny. I think something is wrong."

"What's good, fam'?" Chris asked.

"Ain't nothing good. Where you been? I've been calling since yesterday."

"It was my birthday. Me and Misty went out. Why? What's so urgent?"

"Nigga, Country's dead!"

Chris stood motionless. The earth spun around him. He felt completely separated from the world.

"Baby, what's wrong?" Misty asked. Chris's skin turned pale and his eyes were moist.

Realizing Manny was still on the phone, Chris asked, "What happened?"

"Honestly, I don't know. All I know is I'm not trying to rap on this phone."

"Meet me at Hitches," Chris replied.

"Yo fam', I'm hotter than fish grease right now. How about we meet at the spot we used to play at when we were little. You know where I'm talking about?" asked Manny.

"Yeah. It's gonna take me about a half hour though."

"Whatever. Just hurry up."

Chris hung up with Manny and sat down on the couch. Misty knew whatever happened was bad. "Baby, what's going on?" she asked.

He turned to look at his wife. "Country's dead."

She didn't know how to respond. She cried as she held her husband, trying to offer him some form of comfort. As long as she'd known her husband, he and Country had been friends. From what she knew, the two grew up next to one another, and Chris trusted Country with his life. She knew he was hurting. There was pain in his eyes that she had never seen.

Chris got up off the couch and grabbed his cell phone and keys. He kissed Misty, told her he loved her, and left.

Chris had grown up in the 63 building of Crawford Village. He and Country had lived on the sixth floor. Manny had lived on the first floor. As kids, all of them used to play together near the huge courtyard behind their building littered with trash, broken bottles, and dope fiends. Even the basketball court possessed backboards without rims. A huge fountain shaped like a yellow-fish stood out in the middle of the courtyard that never worked. It did more bad than good, being the eyesore that it was. They made the best of their decrepit environment. In those days, kids weren't allowed in the house during the day. They stayed outside and played until the street lights came on.

The building had long since been closed down. Chris figured that whatever Manny was on the run about, it had him taking shelter somewhere in Crawford.

Chris made it to McKeesport and pulled into the lot that was kitty corner to the old abandoned high rise. He made his way around the structure, and Manny emerged from behind the trees.

"What's up with the cloak and dagger shit?" Chris asked. Manny wanting to meet Chris in the cut, sneaking around and shit made Chris uneasy. Manny could have just told him where he was at and Chris would have come to him.

"'Cause nigga I don't know what the fuck is going on. So I'm not into trusting nobody right now. I know the police are going to be looking for my ass sooner than later."

"So now you don't trust me?" Chris asked.

"No disrespect, fam', but you did shoot me," Manny replied.

"All right, Mann. I feel you. But what's going on?"

Manny began to explain that he and Country were at the mall. Manny was grabbing something to eat in the food court. "Out of nowhere this nigga started dumpin' on us," Manny said.

"Who was he? Was it more than one?" Manny cut Chris's barrage of questions off.

"Nigga, I don't know. Anyway, Country's ass got hit and he's going hard. I ain't never seen no shit like this. Chris, this nigga had about ten bullets in him, and he was still trying to give it to this dude."

"So what was you doing?" Chris asked.

"Motherfucker, I'm shootin', but the dude had the drop on us. He was tucked behind the jewelry kiosk, and we were out in the open. I ducked behind the escalator when he started shooting at us."

"So yinz ain't hit him?"

"Let me finish, nigga, damn! Yeah, that pussy's dead. Nigga, Country put one right in his dome."

"Yo, I can't believe this shit," Chris replied as he put his hands on his head and paced in frustration.

"Man, it gets worse. A little boy got hit," Manny said as he stared at his feet nervously.

"Is he dead?" Chris asked, wondering if their situation could get any worse.

"I watched the news last night and this morning. He was critical."

"They didn't say the name of the boy that tried to hit yinz?"

"No name has been released. But dog, this shit is crazy. They got my description all over the news. Once they release Country's name, someone is gonna put it together."

"Maybe not. I can't believe this shit though," Chris said.

"Dog, I know you're hurtin'. Country was my dude, too. I can't believe he's gone."

Chris just shook his head in disbelief. Country wasn't even twenty years old, and he was gone. He didn't have anybody. All he had was his friends and the streets. Country was Chris's brother. Even though they weren't blood, they were as tight as twins. Now he was gone. No matter what, Chris would make sure that Country went out in style.

"Yo. Man-Man, you good on dough? You need something to lay back for a while so shit can cool down?"

THE DEVIL'S GAME

"I'm good."

"Well, if you need something hit me up. Maybe you should go on vacation or something. I'll take care of this mess up here," Chris said.

"That might be a good idea. And dog, I'm sorry for trippin' on you. This shooting just got me paranoid," Manny stated.

"Don't sweat that shit. I'm gonna head to the Blue Note and catch the news. Be safe." Chris dapped Manny's fist.

"No doubt."

Chris walked away from Manny trying to digest everything. He wanted to know what sparked the shooting. Hopefully, the news would have some more information available to help sort things out.

When Chris walked into the half-empty bar, the news was just coming on. Two patrons were shooting pool and they offered their condolences for Country. Chris thanked them, bought a round of Henny, and then sat down.

The shooting was just coming on the news and Chris sat and listened to the reporter. "Good evening this is John Stewart, and I am Katie Smith and tonight at Century III Mall in Pleasant Hills there was a deadly shooting. Both shooters were pronounced dead on the scene. A ten year-old boy was critically wounded and is currently fighting for his life. Witnesses say that it was like the wild wild west when both gunmen began shooting at each other on the second level of the mall in the food court area. There is a third suspect on the loose. Anyone with any information is asked to call the Allegheny County Police. Anyone who provides information will remain anonymous." As the story continued, Chris silently prayed for the young boy to pull through when they finally released the shooter's name. When Chris heard it, everything fell into place. "Corey Jefferies."

SHAWN 'JIHAD' TRUMP

Chris downed his drink and asked for a double. He had seriously misjudged Corey. The kid wasn't hiding; he was hunting. Chris's arrogance made him assume otherwise, and now his best friend was dead. Country kept talking about dealing with Corey. Chris responded by saying, "That chump is running for his life. He don't want no drama. He saw what happened to his man. Let that faggot sleep and think we don't know. Eventually, he'll think it's safe and show his face. There ain't no reason for you to be wasting your time. When he crawls out of his hole, kill him."

Now Country was dead because Chris didn't take heed to his concern.

Chris heard the door open and looked over to see two police officers enter the establishment. "Hey Donnie, look what the fuck we got here," said Officer Green to his partner.

Chris just looked at the officers, knowing they were about to fuck with him. "What the fuck yinz want?" he asked.

"So what happened, Chris? Did Country come up short? Is that why he's dead?" Detective Green asked.

"You can't be that fucking dumb," Chris replied. It was a statement, not a question.

"Well, maybe you can tell me why he's dead," the detective said.

"412-555-1212. You supposed to call them for information." Chris laughed. Then he placed a serious look on his face and looked into the detectives eyes. "If I knew anything, do you really think I would tell you?"

The detective snatched Chris out of his seat and threw him against the wall. "Your fucking boy is dead, and you think it's a joke. I'm tired of you motherfuckers killing one another!" he screamed.

"Motherfucker, Country didn't even get killed in the hood. It ain't none of your fucking business. Now get your motherfucking hands off me!"

"Or what? You gonna kill me? I'm so fucking scared." The detective laughed.

"Nah, never that. I might just catch that pretty little wife out and put this big white dick in her," Chris replied.

Five minutes later, Chris woke up. "What the fuck?" he said while clutching his head.

The bartender was kneeling next to him trying to help him up. "You were out cold. Green's partner cracked you with his baton. "Here," she said, offering him a towel. "You're bleeding."

Chris looked at his hand smeared with blood that came from the wound on his head. "I'm gonna kill that motherfucker!" he said.

He couldn't understand why Green came in the bar harassing him. Country's murder was in another jurisdiction. Chris hadn't had any legal problems in McKeesport since Manny's shooting. There were a few other boys in McKeesport getting drug money on his level, and he was the least flamboyant of them all. This motherfucker was making shit personal.

Chris stayed at the bar. The cut on his head didn't require stitches. The bartender cleaned it up for him. By his fourth Henny he didn't feel a thing. On the eighth drink he was calling Misty's mother, Beverly, who lived a few minutes away to come and get him.

When she walked in the bar and saw Chris, the first words out of her mouth were, "Son, you look like shit."

"Thanks a lot," Chris slurred.

"Baby, I know you're hurting. We all loved Country, but keep in mind you're the rock in your family's life. Your wife needs you and so does your child. The best thing you can do for Country is walk away. Trust me when I tell you these streets don't love nobody."

He tried to hold back his tears, but it was to no avail. The tears began to flow. Beverly held him close. She had never seen her son-in-law cry. Everybody had a breaking point and Chris had reached his.

Chris's tears were the result of multiple things. Murder, and not just Country's, but the murders of Quick, Rico, and Richey. The malice he had been a part of replayed itself in his sleep. He cried because he felt helpless, like he was nothing without the streets. Without them, he believed he couldn't survive. He cried for his wife and unborn child. He provided them with money and love, but there was absolutely no security. How could they depend on a man who was so selfish that he would place himself in a position to be taken away from them at any moment? His mother. What did she have to be proud of? Her son was a monster who funneled death into the community. He wanted to get out. His money was plentiful. There was no one left to avenge. Everyone who crossed him was gone. If he didn't do it now he might never walk away. All he had to do was get rid of the rest of his work and let Val know he was done.

The only problem was that things were a mess. Chris had five kilos left. He could give them to Benny and be done, but he had given Country ten kilos. Five of them went to Manny. Chris now had to find what coke was left and any money Country might have left behind. He assumed Manny had paid Country, but forgot to ask Manny about it when he last saw him. If by chance Manny hadn't paid yet, Chris would have to count it as a loss anyway. How could he ask for the money with Manny being on the run? Especially when it stemmed from an incident that Manny had nothing to do with. What type of man would that make Chris? The only thing Chris could do now was go by Country's home and see what was left behind. Whatever loss he would take he would just have to suck it up and move on.

Misty's mother walked Chris to her truck and helped him in. When they got to her home, Chris went straight to Misty's old room and passed out. Misty's mother followed behind him, took off his boots, and covered him up. She then retired to the living room and called her daughter.

When Misty answered, her mom informed her that she had picked him up at the Blue Note and that he was pretty drunk. She didn't forget to mention how the police smacked him in his hard ass head with something.

"What? Is he all right?" Misty asked, becoming worried.

"Baby, your husband is one person who will always be all right. He just needs to rest. You're welcome to come join him. I'll even cook your favorite meal."

"For some fried chicken and mac & cheese I'd fly to a third world country right now. I'm on my way," Misty said with a chuckle.

CHAPTER 18

When Chris opened his eyes and saw Misty's room he was relieved. "I must have been dreaming. Yo, that shit was crazy," he said.

Misty lay next to him. He snuggled up close to her and put his arm around her. "What the fuck?" he hollered as his wife jumped out of bed.

"Baby, what's wrong?" she asked.

"You're pregnant?" he said.

Misty was confused as Chris began to babble. "It was a dream. Country ain't dead. It's got to be a dream," Chris said.

In his confused mind, Misty was still in high school, and the last few years of his life weren't real. Waking up in Misty's room threw Chris's sense of reality completely off.

Misty began to cry as she held her husband, scared that he was going to lose his mind from everything he was going through.

"Why are we at your mom's?" Chris asked, snapping back into reality.

"You were drunk and called her, papi," she answered.

"Damn," Chris said as he explained to Misty why he was tripping.

She was relieved to know that he wasn't losing his mind. He had been through so much. She had no idea how he was going to deal with it.

It was a little after nine at night when Chris woke up. Beverly warmed up his plate while Misty helped him to the table.

While devouring the food, he told Misty that he had to go to Country's house. She didn't want him to be alone, so she offered to drive him. He accepted her offer.

They drove to Country's home in silence. When they pulled into the driveway Chris screamed, "Stop the car!"

Parked next to the house was a black Cadillac Deville. It wasn't Country's car, and nobody but Chris knew where Country lived. He wouldn't even invite a woman to his home. He would take her to a hotel. Seeing an unfamiliar car in the driveway had Chris on high alert.

"Baby, I want you to pull up the road. I'll call your cell when I want you to come back."

"Papi, what's wrong?" she asked.

"Just do it!" Chris said firmly. He jumped out of the car and walked toward the house. He noticed the front door was ajar. He reached under the seat and retrieved his pistol.

The house was dark. Chris entered cautiously and went room to room looking for the owner of the Caddy. He was halfway through the living room when he heard the unmistakable sound of a round being chambered.

"I knew you would be here sooner or later," said the man sitting on the couch.

The darkness didn't allow Chris a view of the man, but he knew the voice. An outside light illuminated the polished steel of the man's firearm.

Sensing Chris's uncertainty, the gun wielding man turned on the light by the couch.

"Green?" said Chris, shocked to see the detective sitting on Country's couch. In front of him on the table was a bottle of E&J. He was clearly drunk.

"What the fuck?" Chris asked.

"Drop the gun, Chris," said the detective.

Chris put down the gun and raised his hands. The detective could see the confusion on his face. *What the fuck is going on?* Chris thought.

"Chris, I want to be real clear about something. Officially, I'm not here. This is all personal. So if you don't tell me what I want to know I won't hesitate to kill you."

"What? You here trying to get paid or something?" Chris asked.

Green laughed out loud. "Do you remember Country's mother?"

"Yeah. She and my mom was always cool. What does that got to do with anything?"

"Did you know that Jackie and I were high school sweethearts? She was a fine woman. Crazy as all hell, but damn she was fine. Anyway, I joined the military and got sent overseas. When I enlisted we had a huge argument. I said a lot of things I shouldn't have. I left without making amends. Then I found out that she got pregnant and had a son. She never told me I was the father so I assumed it was by someone else."

"Country," Chris stated the obvious.

"Exactly. Anyway, I was mad as hell. I'm away serving my country and she is back here making babies. So I never tried to hook back up with her. I met my wife and forgot all about Jackie."

"So now what? You're trying to prove your love to Jackie or something? I don't think that's gonna work, detective. Miss Jackie been dead almost five years. And why you telling me all this anyway?"

"I never asked Jackie about her son. I found out about him and wrote her a letter calling her a bunch of low down whores and what not. She and I never spoke after that. That is until she was dying. You see, Jackie wasn't back here whoring around. If I wouldn't have been so immature and asked her about Country instead, I would have found out twenty years ago that I had a son."

Chris's eyes grew wide. "You're Country's dad?"

"That's right, Chris. And he died without knowing. Now nobody knows but the two of us. And if you don't explain to me why my son is dead then only I will know. You feel me?"

Chris felt him. Now he knew why Green was taking this shit so personal. Chris was left with two choices—try to feed the detective a bullshit story or tell the truth. The latter gave him a better chance of walking out of the door alive. Telling the detective about Richey's murder wasn't rational, but it was the basis of Corey's actions. Would the detective implicate Chris? He would take that chance. He was tired of carrying all of this shit around.

Chris started from the beginning. From the day Richey and Corey tried to rob them till the meeting at the mall. The only thing he kept secret was Manny's identity, but the detective filled in the blank.

The detective looked at Chris after he finished and set his gun down. Without saying a word, he grabbed a bag off the floor and tossed it at Chris. "I know you and him were like brothers. I found that in the closet. He would want you to have it," he said.

SHAWN 'JIHAD' TRUMP

Chris opened the bag, but the detective interrupted him. "Five-hundred twenty thousand dollars. There were two kilos of cocaine that I destroyed. You're done with this game. Chris, I'm tired of seeing you kids throw your lives away. Take what money you have and walk away."

Chris was dumbfounded and unsure about the situation he found himself in. He knew that trying to explain that he had every intention of walking away was frivolous. He turned to leave, but paused before taking another step. I loved your son like my blood. He was the most loyal person I have ever met."

The detective broke down in tears as Chris walked out the door and called Misty to come and get him.

CHAPTER 19

Country's viewing was held at Water's funeral home in McKeesport. Over two hundred people were in attendance. Very few of them knew Country well. All the ballers came out to pay their respect. Anytime a soldier was slain in the streets, hustlers came out to show homage. However, it seemed to be more of a fashion show than a viewing.

A group of brothers passed a bottle of Crown Royal between themselves. They were dressed in some loud ass colors, drawing the stares of everyone in the funeral home. One of the brothers wore a thick chain with an enormous diamond encrusted cross. Females walked around with their asses on display in short "hoochie mama" dresses. *They don't have no fucking respect for themselves,* Chris thought.

"What the fuck? Are we at the club or something?" Chris spat so Misty could hear him.

Chris was further disturbed that Val had come through and pretended that Country's death had some type of effect on her emotions. The only thing that bitch cared about was the money. It was proven when she asked to speak with him outside.

"So how you holding up?" she inquired.

"I'm cool," Chris said, not offering much.

"I know you're going through a lot right now, and I hate to be hollering at you about business, but I need to know where we stand."

I can't believe this bitch! Chris wanted to cuss her out and walk away, but he didn't want to burn any bridges. If being legit didn't work out he would need her.

"Val, I gotta lay back for a minute. I've lost Country. Manny is laying low. Benny can only move so much. I'm gonna drop these last five I got on Benny and lay back until Misty has the baby. Shit needs to cool down. Let the law think that I went straight," said Chris.

Val was unconvinced, but she played along. Her operation with Chris in Pittsburgh was small in her family's overall scheme, but it let her live well. Her father wouldn't care if he lost Chris. He would be more than happy to see Val lose him, so she would have to get out of the business. Chris was the only one of Jesus's customers whom Val really knew. Without him she would have to build her own clientele, which meant trusting someone. Val wasn't having it. Chris would play ball, or she would take him out the game for good. She would let it play out and see what happened. Misty was due at the beginning of August, which was less than three months away. Val had enough loot to lay back for a minute.

"Okay baby," she said and rubbed her hand across his crotch. "Just don't be a stranger."

Chris walked away. Val made him sick to his stomach. *How could Jesus have trusted that bitch so much?* He made his way back inside the funeral home and stood by Misty.

The rest of the night was a blur. Chris was deep in thought replaying his life. It seemed like yesterday he and Country were having sleepovers. They would build tents out of their blankets and act like they were camping. To them, riding their bikes or playing tag was the greatest thing in the world. Money was the furthest thing from their mind. Somewhere along the line everything changed. Life became more sinister. They became addicted to the streets. In this game if you got tagged you went to your grave or prison.

After the viewing, Chris and Misty left the funeral home and drove to Beverly's house. The funeral was the next morning, so there was no reason to travel all the way to their home. They ate a late dinner and sat up talking until they made their way to the bedroom. Lying in bed with Misty, Chris realized how valuable life really was. He held her tight, scared to let go. Country's death had taught him that tomorrow was never promised. There was so much he wished he could do and say, but he would never get that chance. He wouldn't make that mistake with Misty and his child. He would love them like every day was their last, so there would be no regrets. Before he fell asleep, he kissed his wife and told her he loved her.

Chris tossed and turned all night. He awoke around 6 a.m. and made everyone breakfast. Misty and her mother joined him. They ate and then got ready for the funeral.

Chris was asked to give the eulogy. He didn't know about a eulogy, but for sure he definitely wanted to say a few words for his home boy. He took the podium. "Country was more than my friend. He was my brother. I remember growing up I was one of the only white kids in our building, and I stayed fighting to prove myself. I was little as hell, so Country was always jumping in to help me." Everyone smiled, thinking about the two inseparable youths.

"Country never left my side. I never left his. We did everything together. Damn, we even got shot together. Any pain I've ever felt, he was by my side to feel it with me. Even though I didn't die the day that he did, a part of me still died too. I will never be able to replace his loyalty toward me. In my heart, I believe no man, including myself, compares to the man that Country was."

By the time Chris finished, his eyes were full of tears. People embraced him as he walked back to his wife. They started to leave when Chris noticed Detective Green in the back of the room. At first glance, the man appeared to be stoic, but Chris knew that deep inside the detective's heart was in pieces. Chris stopped and shook the man's hand. "Thank you for coming," he said.

The detective nodded. Just like Chris, he was blaming himself for Country's death. If only he would have approached his son sooner and told him. Maybe Country wouldn't be lying in a box. He had been scared to tell his wife and other son. Even though it had happened before they met, his wife was a jealous woman. Now he was full of regret. Country shouldn't have been left in the world to live alone without a father to guide him. Green felt like a coward. There was nothing he could do to make things right with Country. He gave Chris a chance and prayed that he would take it. Then Country's death wouldn't be in vain. Green thought that if he could save Chris from the streets then it would offer him some sort of redemption.

Chris, Benny, and four of Country's young boys were pallbearers. Chris had attempted to track down Country's family without success. Miss Jackie was an only child. Her parents were both dead. Country's only family was the brothers in the streets whom he ran with day in and day out. He had asked Detective Green to be a pallbearer, but he declined, saying, "That's an honor I don't deserve. I never opened my mouth, so he died thinking of me as an enemy."

It was a small procession. Chris rented two Rolls Royce limos. One for him, Misty, her mother Beverly, and Benny and the other was for the young boys. Country was always talking about them. Their names were Jihad, Crook, Teku, and Tree. He loved the young boys to death. They weren't much younger. Jihad and Crook were eighteen and Teku and Tree were both seventeen. He always said Jihad reminded him of Chris. "The only white boy I know besides you who be putting his thing down in the hood." Chris had to laugh. Jihad and Crook looked exactly like him and Country when they were coming up. He made a mental note to take care of them after everything was said and done.

The funeral was short. It only lasted an hour. Afterward, a gathering was held at Tambelini's on Route 51. Only about twenty people attended. Chris had vowed to send Country off in style. Dom Perignon, along with every other kind of liquor was poured like water into their glasses. Food was served in abundance, and the group ate until they were ready to bust. Everyone in attendance got wasted, and by the end of the night the mood was festive as they rejoiced in Country's memory. When Chris staggered out the party, he smiled knowing that one day he would join Country. Chris turned his bottle upside down and poured out his champagne and said, "See you in hell, baby boy."

CHAPTER 20

A few months had passed since Country's death. On August 2, Misty gave birth to a baby girl. They named her Autumn. Seeing Misty give birth transformed Chris instantly. It was something about becoming a father. For the first time in his life, there was someone Chris cared about more than himself. He loved Misty and viewed her as his equal. However, his daughter was angelic. Looking at her, he knew there was a God. Her innocence hypnotized him. The moment she escaped from her mother's womb he was under her spell.

Up until that point, Chris had failed to leave the game alone. He had sat down with Country's young boys, Jihad and Crook and realized just how much potential they really had. The financial void of Country's death was easily filled. This had Val elated. After a two-week hiatus following Country's death, Chris had called her with an order.

"I thought you were chillin'?" she had said.

"Yeah, me too, but fuck it. I might as well get it while it's out here," Chris replied.

With Country gone, he and Benny started to kick it a little more. Benny began to fill Country's shoes as Chris's right hand man. This didn't sit well with Manny, who came out of hiding when no warrants had been issued for his arrest for the incident at the mall.

Chris and Manny had grown up in the same hood. They were always cool but had never been everyday friends. The fact that Chris had shot him had diminished trust in Chris's mind. He was always conscious that Manny might one day try to pay him back. On top of these issues, Manny was extremely flashy. Everybody knew what Manny did for a living. He didn't try to hide anything. He was proud to be a drug dealer. He drove a new BMW, wore excessive jewelry, and never acted like he had a job. Chris would at least lie and tell people he worked. Chris had made it a habit to be in and out of the hood. He didn't turn his back on the hood, but he learned from seeing other people get jammed up that flaunting money in the hood was a quick way to prison or a grave.

Benny was an older cat. He and Jesus had been tight. Even though Chris had more money, Benny's knowledge and values were priceless. Chris learned a lot from him. Chris had spoken to Benny a few times about his desire to get away from the drug game. Benny encouraged him to do so.

"You got your whole life ahead of you. If I was you I'd be done too," Benny remarked.

Chris realized how selfless Benny's words were. Most drug dealers would have tried to coerce him into never leaving.

Benny would have left the game alone, but an armed robbery conviction that occurred shortly after high school prevented him from, in his mind, obtaining gainful employment. Although Benny was a very intelligent individual and possessed uncanny street smarts, he wasn't confident in his ability to start a legitimate business. This was the case with many young men in the hood.

Since becoming a father, Chris was being torn apart from the inside out. For the first time in his life, Chris was scared to go to prison. But he wasn't going to just walk away. He was going to put one more move down and make sure everyone in his life was straight.

He put the call in to Val and went to see her. After putting in his order, she looked at him like he was crazy.

"A hundred what?" Val asked.

"What the fuck you mean 'a hundred what'? You know what I want," Chris said.

"I can't bring you no hundred kilos. I can't fit but so many in the spot. And I ain't riding with that shit if it ain't tucked away."

Val was doing the math in her head. One hundred kilos was $1.8 million. One hundred thousand would be hers. She became leery the more she thought about it. Chris had never purchased more than thirty kilos. *Why the drastic increase? Robbery? Was it a set up?*

"So, why so many?" she asked.

"'Cause I need to be spending time with my wife and daughter. I'm gonna stockpile that shit and let my people do their thing. Every week I gotta stop what I'm doing to get at you."

"I'll speak with my family, but I can't promise nothing though," she said.

"It's cool. By the way, I'd hate to pay eighteen a piece if I'm buying a hundred at a time," he said.

Val laughed. "I'll see what I can do." She was now somewhat relieved that Chris's sudden increase was probably attributed to getting a better price. She knew that getting him the hundred kilos wouldn't be a problem. Her father, a prominent attorney who co-founded one of New York's elite law firm, had married a young Russian woman. They had attended Harvard together. Her father later found out the woman he loved was the daughter of Nicholai Storsky, a top lieutenant in the Russian mafia operating under the control of The Don "Semion Mogilevich."

The money Val's father made representing some of New York's most notorious criminals was peanuts compared to the drug money he made working for Nicholai. In charge of all drug trafficking in the region, Val's father utilized his position as an attorney to recruit and establish new partnerships with all the major drug dealers. He had tried to shield Val from the game, but she was attracted to bad guys like a gangsta to a gun. She loved the power that the game gave her. She was Nicholai through and through.

In reality, Val didn't need the money. Her father would give her anything, but she hated to ask. Her pride fueled her desire to pave her own road. Combined with her beauty, brains, and love for money, she was extremely conniving, which made her a very powerful woman to reckon with. The control she had over men only fueled her power hunger. Her father had given up reasoning with her while she was still a teenager.

The day after Val met with Chris, she strolled into her father's law office. He looked up, surprised.

"Hey princess. What are you doing here?" he asked as he rose to give his daughter a hug.

"Can't a girl come see her father at work?" she asked.

"Of course, of course. So why are you really here?" he asked.

She smiled and took a seat at her father's desk. Then, without wasting any more time, she replayed her conversation with Chris. Her father looked at her skeptically and asked, "Do you trust him?"

"Yes. Chris is a standup guy. He believes in all that loyalty and values crap."

"What about his cases?"

"Petty. His lawyer got him a plea for probation on one charge. The second one he is pleading to is six to twenty-three months. The judge is going to suspend the sentence. He won't do a day in jail."

"Good, I had been wondering about the pending cases he had. But listen, your brother will bring the shipment and I want him there during the transaction."

"No, this is *my* deal. I don't need Peter there," she protested.

"This is not negotiable. I'll pay Peter, so you'll make your money. Tell Christopher I'll take a thousand dollars off each kilo. That is the best I can do for him."

Protesting any further would have been in vain. Val stood and embraced her father. "When will it arrive?" she asked.

"This weekend. And princess, be careful. I still worry that Chris will find out that you double-crossed Jesus. What you do in the dark always comes to light, and I'm sure he will seek retribution for his friend."

"How would he find out?" Val asked.

"Never underestimate people, Valerie. I've told you that. I still don't understand why you did what you did? And that business with his uncle Rico was unnecessary. Jesus was a good man and wanted to walk away from all of this nonsense. He wanted to take you with him."

"Daddy, I don't want to talk about this right now. I loved Jesus, but walking away from our family's business was a weakness I was not willing to tolerate. He didn't leave me any choice and his uncle had to go. Rico was already asking me questions as soon as I got released from the Feds custody. He knew things weren't adding up, and I couldn't answer his questions. Rico and I were the only two people that knew Jesus and I were making that trip. He knew we had been fighting. He was the reason Jesus was getting out of the game, filling his head with all that bullshit," she replied defensively.

Val hated discussing Jesus. Since he went to prison she had been alone. No man had been able to meet her standards. She sent the one man she had truly loved to prison, but she couldn't allow love to get in the way of her money.

They had argued during their trip to New York. Jesus had told her his plans, which involved him leaving the drug game. She remembered the conversation as if it were yesterday. "This is my last trip, baby, and I'm done. I'm gonna speak to Chris when we get back. He's a good kid, and I don't want to see him end up dead or in prison."

"Well, what do you plan on doing, Jesus?" she demanded.

"I'm going to open a restaurant," he replied.

"That's just fucking stupid! You never did nothin' legit in your life. Now all of a sudden you want to chase your dreams. Jesus, this is all we know. What kind of life will we have with a stupid restaurant? I refuse to be running to my father for money because you can't give me what I need," she had spat.

Instead of supporting her husband, Val had chastised him. "We won't ever make any real money legitimately. You're talking like a fucking punk! Why don't you grow some balls?"

Out of anger Val tipped off the Feds. She had called them before they got on the highway. She never considered the consequences of her actions. She could have jeopardized her whole family.

SHAWN 'JIHAD' TRUMP

The Feds had arrested her to make things look good. Concealing their informant was ironically made easy by Jesus's chivalry. He didn't even try to fight. He pled guilty in return for Val's freedom without knowing that Val's charges would have never made it to trial.

Now, thanks to her father, Val wondered if Chris had somehow found out about her treason and planned to rob and kill her. She was suddenly glad that Peter would be there. He was no killer, or nowhere near as ruthless as Chris, but if something happened, Peter would have the element of surprise in his favor.

"Be safe, Daddy. I love you," Val said. She quickly escaped from her father's office and headed back to Pittsburgh.

Val's father watched her leave. He hated seeing his daughter mixed up in Nicholai's criminal enterprise. He knew that one day her ways would bring her death, but there was little he could do to prevent it. If he cut her off she would run straight to Nicholai. His father-in-law's only concern was money. He was actually proud that his grandchildren had chosen to follow in his footsteps. Val's father tried to speak with him a few times but Nicholai wouldn't hear his concerns. He would dismiss him, saying, "You should smile. Your kids are strong. They are survivors. Just like me."

CHAPTER 21

C hris pulled his car in front of Val's home. The sun had just fallen behind the horizon and painted the sky with hues of red and yellow. The fiery image set a hellish scene. Chris thought of the old cliché "making a deal with the devil" and laughed nervously as he got out the car. He retrieved the money from his trunk and went inside.

As usual, Val greeted him warmly and offered him a drink. Chris began to pile the money on the kitchen table. There were one hundred and seventy stacks of ten thousand dollar increments. The sight of all the money made Val's hormones race. She knew that Chris was tight as hell with his money. He always saved more than he spent. But seeing the money on the table made her realize that if Chris had $1.7 million on the table, there was probably that much or more stashed away. Instead of thinking about business, Val was thinking about what she could do to make Chris her man. He was just what she was looking for to fill the void in her life.

Reality was, Chris had his life on the table. The money Detective Green had given him combined with his savings had made Chris a wealthy man. Deep down he knew he should have just walked away, but one more flip wouldn't hurt.

"We gonna do this or what?" Chris asked, bringing Val out of her zone.

Val responded by handing Chris his drink and leading him into the living room.

"Those are yours," Val said, pointing toward the boxes in the corner.

Chris proceeded to the boxes and opened the first one. There were five boxes in all with twenty kilos each. Chris didn't trust Val much. He did, however, trust her product, so without inspecting the stamped packages he began carrying them to his car. Once he got them loaded, he went inside to make sure him and Val were straight.

"We good?" he asked Val.

"We're always good, baby," she replied as she tried to fondle Chris's manhood through his jeans. She didn't even care that her brother was in the guest room waiting to pounce at the first sign of trouble.

"I ain't that drunk," Chris said as he pulled her hand away and began to walk out the door.

"Some other time," Val said, trying to hide the anger in her voice. She couldn't understand how Chris could dismiss her so effortlessly.

Peter walked into the kitchen and said, "You really are scandalous. I know you weren't out here making moves on your husband's good friend?" Peter questioned.

Unlike her father, Peter knew nothing about Val having set up Jesus. Peter always liked Jesus and still talked to him every now and again.

"Peter, Jesus ain't coming home any time soon. I'm too young to be tied down by a man in prison."

"Sis, I understand that. That is not my issue. The issue is, who you are trying to replace Jesus with." Peter walked away from Val.

Fuck him! Val thought. She knew what she did went beyond disgraceful. In her mind, the only way to survive was to combat any weakness. Ever since she was young, Nicholai embedded the motto "by all means necessary" in her mind and made sure she strived to always have her way. To make people bend to her will. She would now do whatever she had to do to achieve her goals, regardless of how shameful they might be. So if she wanted Chris, she would have him. Or nobody would.

Chris was starting to realize just how low down and dirty Val was. He drove his product to his storage unit thinking about Val's advances. Jesus usually called once a month. Every time he asked about Val, Chris felt like shit. He wanted to tell Jesus about Val, but didn't want to jeopardize their friendship. Telling Jesus would be frivolous.

Chris pulled into the unit and began to store the cocaine. After putting up the drugs, he retrieved his phone and called Benny. He answered on the fourth ring.

"Yo."

"What you doing?" Chris asked.

"Having dinner with my mom and sis."

"That's what's up. You think you can get away and meet me at Hitches in an hour?"

"I'm there. Is everything all right?" Benny asked.

"Never been better," Chris replied as he hung up the phone and headed to the bar.

The drive only took about twenty minutes, so he ordered a double Henny and waited for Benny's arrival. While waiting, Chris and the bartender, Trent chatted. The conversation drifted to Chris inquiring about opening a business. Trent was the bar owner's son and was able to brief Chris on the aspects of starting a business.

"Let me find out you're finally getting smart and leaving the game alone," Trent said.

"That's my plan," Chris replied.

The two continued their conversation until Benny finally walked in. Chris stood, and the two men made their way to a table. They took a seat and ordered some food. Chris ordered Benny a drink and another for himself. Like any Saturday night, the bar started to fill up with patrons. Chris wanted to hurry up and get their business out the way.

"What's up?" asked Benny.

"Yo fam', you know you're my man, right?" Chris asked.

"No doubt. Is something wrong?" Benny asked.

"Nah fam'. I told you on the phone that everything is gravy. It's just . . . I gotta get out this game."

"I feel you, fam'. We already spoke about this though. So I know you didn't call me down here to chat about this."

"Kinda. For me to get out I need a favor. I want to make sure you, Manny, and the young boys is cool. To do that I had to gamble a little. I used almost everything I had to cop. So now I need to flip this shit quick to get my paper back. Then I can walk away," Chris informed him.

"You ain't saying nothing, fam'. I got you. How much work you talking about?"

"A hundred joints," Chris said.

Benny spit his drink out all over the table. "Is you serious?"

"As a heart attack. Look, usually I charge yinz $22,500. I just want $20,000 back from you on each one. I need you to fuck with Manny and the young boys. Let them know this is it.

They need to stack their dough and start looking for a connect."

"What about Val?" Benny asked.

Chris hesitated. Val introduced Chris to Benny. Benny still frequently talked to Jesus. He didn't want to slander Val in front of Benny and have him running back to tell Jesus. However, he couldn't avoid an explanation, so he had to take his chances.

"Fam', she's a fucking snake. I don't trust her," Chris replied.

"What do you mean 'you don't trust her'? That's your main man's wife. Everything you got, everything we got is because of her, for real. She didn't have to continue working for Jesus but she did."

"Dog, she ain't working for Jesus. The shit is coming from her family. She was Jesus's connect. And she don't give a fuck about Jesus. Trust me," Chris said.

"I still can't understand why you don't trust her. We been doing business with her for a minute and she never crossed you yet. What did she do to get on your bad side?"

Left without a choice, Chris explained everything except Rico's murder, but included the part about him and her fucking.

Benny shook his head. "Nigga, you know you're wrong as hell."

"I already know that, fam'. I fucked up, but you know I don't get down like that," Chris said defensively.

"I feel you, but what does any of this have to do with business? She always does good business."

"Yeah, she does. But I just got this feeling. When she don't get her way she is scandalous."

"That's cool and all, but if you plug me up with her then you don't have to worry. I just need you to hook it up."

Chris realized that he had said too much. Benny didn't know Val very well. He was becoming defensive. Chris thought about the hundred kilos in storage and redirected the conversation.

"All right, fam', you're right. I can't make no promises though. She's funny about that shit. Let's worry about these hundred joints we got right now, and we'll talk about Val later."

"That's cool. When do you want to get together?" Benny asked.

"I'll swing by your spot in the morning. I'll give you twenty at that time. I want you to holla at the young boys though. They are getting money. If you let them know we got some serious weight they'll go hard," Chris said.

"What about Manny?"

"Five at a time. He's too flashy, so frontin' him too much weight is a risk. But make sure you let everyone know to stack their paper 'cause I mean it this time . . . I'm done."

"All right, fam', I'm with you. So what's your plan for tonight?"

"That bottle of Henny on the shelf. Misty is staying at her mom's with Autumn tonight. She told me I was getting on her nerves. That I needed a boys' night out." Chris laughed.

The two men enjoyed the rest of the night throwing back drinks and talking shit. Benny left around 11 p.m. Chris was finishing his drink in an attempt to follow Benny's lead when Val walked through the door wearing a pair of jeans that fit her body like a glove. Her white Prada blouse was buttoned just below her breasts, exposing her bra, which held her perfect tits firmly in place. Her nails and toes were French manicured. She wore white heels with straps that criss-crossed her feet. It irritated Chris that his dick had a mind of its own and jumped to attention.

"Is this my seat?" Val asked. Every person in the bar turned their attention toward her. Men were lusting and women hated.

"It's a free country," Chris replied.

"Wow, I feel so welcome," Val said sarcastically.

"You don't never come down here. So what's up?"

"Nothing is up. You just made me a hundred grand, so I figured I would come out and spend some of it."

"You just made a hundred grand, and you chose to go out by yourself to Hitches." He tried not to mask his humor.

"You really are an arrogant motherfucker. Always thinkin' it's about Chris." She smiled.

"No, I just know Val."

"And what do you know?"

"I know that you ain't gonna fuck no ordinary muhfucker. If a brother ain't got no serious paper then he can't get at you. And I know that I'm that dude you're trying to get at. The thing is, baby girl. I love mine. I'm not fucking that up for you or anybody."

Val just shook her head and smiled. "You wasn't saying nothing when you was fucking me on my table. Don't act like you didn't like that shit."

"Look, the pussy is mean and you's a fly motherfucker. But that shit was a mistake. All we did was fuck, and it was the first and last time."

Chris got up to leave. This bitch wasn't getting the point. He made it out the door and to his car. Her heels click clacked behind him. Chris got into his car and she jumped in the passenger seat.

"Don't you ever fucking walk away from me! You better get with the program. I get what the fuck I want! You belong to *me*, motherfucker! If I want to fuck you, best believe you gonna drop those jeans and fuck me. I made your ass. Without me you wouldn't be shit. I'll cut you off and put your ass in prison with Jesus. Then I'll go visit that pretty little wife of —"

Chris reached across the console and snatched Val by the neck. "Bitch, who the fuck you think you're talking to?" Chris nearly choked the life out of her as Val struggled to breathe. It took him a second to realize what was happening. He let go and she grabbed the handle trying to escape.

"Motherfucker, you're dead! You fucked with the wrong bitch!" Val hollered. Then she added, "Jesus crossed me and I sent his ass to prison, but you're going to your fucking grave. Then I'm sending your wife and kid to join you!"

Val's words struck like lightning, and Chris realized just how low she was. Val had put her husband in prison and slept with his main man. For what, he didn't know. He didn't care. Only one thing could happen now. In three seconds he was around the car and on her. She fumbled inside her purse, reaching for her gun. Her attempt was cut short as he threw a quick punch that shattered her jaw. She crumbled to the pavement. Chris hurriedly retrieved her keys and popped the trunk to her brand new S500 Mercedes Benz. He made sure nobody was watching in the scarcely lit parking lot. He grabbed her limp body and tossed her in the trunk. Then he locked his car, jumped behind the wheel of her car, and sped out of the parking lot. His plan formulated as he drove toward her home. Chris had been driving for five minutes when Val regained consciousness and began banging on the trunk lid and trying to kick through the backseat. The last thing he needed was to get pulled over with her in the trunk. He would never see the light of day again. Val knew enough to put him under the prison.

He made it to her house without incident. As he pulled beside the house and cut the engine, her voice became clear.

"Let me the fuck out of here!" she screamed.

Chris jumped out of the vehicle and proceeded to the rear of the car. When he hit the button and the trunk opened, Chris had to duck as Val slung a small dumb bell at his head. The weight grazed his head causing him to lose his footing. He quickly regained his balance and caught Val by the hair as she tried to scurry out of the trunk. She only managed to get one leg out. Chris yanked her with so much force that her body lifted horizontally and she landed with a bone-jarring thud three-feet from the vehicle. The wind left her body and she fought for her breath once again.

"Pl-please," she begged.

Chris didn't answer her. Instead, he dragged her across the driveway and up the front steps with one hand. Using his free hand, he unlocked her door and dragged her inside.

Val knew she was in trouble. Her confession and threat were not intentional. She was infuriated that Chris rejected her so easily. She assumed her family's status would prevent Chris from harming her. The truth was, Chris didn't know much about Val's family. If he would have, his path may have been different. He might have given her a pass, but his ignorance sealed Val's fate.

He pulled her in the living room and threw her in the corner like a sack of potatoes. Chris raised his pistol and screamed, "He was your fucking husband! Bitch! He fucking loved you!"

His words were venomous. Val stared up at him stoically. She knew she was going to die. Chris was unforgiving to those who crossed him. "If you're going to kill me then do it. Quit fucking talking. Because as soon as you pull that trigger it will be your funeral along with everyone you love," she threatened.

Chris pulled the trigger and continued to pull it as her body jerked with every piece of hot lead that tore through her flesh. The clip had gone empty, but he continued to squeeze.

"Fuck!" Chris screamed, knowing he'd fucked up. Val's death would bring certain drama. Her family would want revenge, and he was sure to be a suspect. *They can't prove shit,* he kept telling himself as he quickly pulled himself together and went to work. The first thing he did was look for the money. He tore the house upside down, but all he found was a few grand that Val had tucked away in her purse. Chris knew it had to be somewhere, but he didn't know where to look. He pulled pictures off the wall, lifted carpets looking for a safe but found nothing. In the end he decided that the money wasn't important. He needed to clean the place and Val's car of any traces that might connect him to the murder.

Chris spent the next hour and a half wiping everything down in her house that he had ever touched. He was just finishing up when Misty pulled in the driveway. Chris walked out the door and got into her vehicle. As soon as he sat in the car, Misty started to scream, "What the fuck you doing at this bitch's crib at three in the morning? And you got the nerve to call me for a ride!"

Chris tried to control his tone. "Misty, if I was doing something with Val I wouldn't have called your ass. So please be quiet for a second."

"Christopher, what the hell is going on?" she asked.

"Look mama, just get us out of here. I'll explain everything when we get to the house.

Chris didn't want to involve Misty. There was nobody else he could call to come get him though. Taking Val's car wasn't an option. He didn't want to chance getting pulled over or being seen in it. He had exposed himself enough in Hitches parking lot and silently prayed that no one witnessed the altercation. Right now, Misty was the only person he trusted completely, and he needed her support more than ever.

They made it home. Once inside, Misty sat at the dining room table. Chris sat on the opposite side facing her. She didn't speak, but sat quietly and waited for Chris to explain.

"It's complicated," Chris said, trying to ease his way into the conversation.

"Uncomplicate it," Misty said, crossing her arms.

"Val's dead," Chris said bluntly.

"What!" Misty bit her knuckle. Her eyes began to water. "What happened?"

Chris told her about Val's sneaky ways, but he omitted Rico's death and his indiscretion with Val in order to save his ass. He ended the story with Val's confession at the bar and how she went for her gun.

Misty stared at her husband in shock.

"Papi, what did you do?"

"What I had to do," Chris replied coldly. "That bitch was gonna either kill me or put me in prison. She put Jesus in prison. She was gonna try to hurt you. What the fuck was I supposed to do?"

"I don't know, but you can't just kill people," she said through tears.

Chris tried to respond, but Misty got up from the table and ran to the bedroom. Chris followed her. She lay on the bed with her back to him. He sat down on the edge of the bed and put his hand on her shoulder.

"Papi, it has to stop. I can't do it anymore. You have to stop," she pleaded.

"I know, mama. I know," he replied.

"I mean it, Christopher. It's me and Autumn or the streets. I love you with all my heart, but I can't accept you doing this anymore."

"I know, baby girl. I swear, as soon as I clean out the storage unit, I'm done."

"Well, when you're done doing that you're welcome in our home again. Until then, you can get out."

"Huh?" Chris could not believe his ears.

"You heard me, Christopher. As long as you're in the streets you won't be under this roof. Our *daughter's* roof. You can't even go out for the night and not get into something. You were supposed to have a boys' night out. Instead, you call me at my mom's at 2 a.m. to come pick you up because you just killed someone. This ain't normal. I can't live like this, Christopher, so please just get out."

Chris stared at his wife's back, stunned.

"Are you giving me an ultimatum?" he asked, more shocked than angry.

She turned to look at him. "Papi, I'm giving you an opportunity to show me how much we mean to you. Can you buy another family with all that money?"

"Mama, you know the answer. But it ain't that simple. I just gave Val almost two million dollars today. Almost all our money. I planned on going thru this package and quitting."

"Christopher, you're always saying it's your last time."

"I promise. This one last run and I'm done."

"What about Val? Is this gonna come back on us?"

"Nobody really knows Val. I scrubbed the house. Only Benny knows her. Her family might have some questions, but nothing can lead back to me. I know she checked in since I saw her today, so they will know I didn't rob her. I just grabbed enough work for the next month, so there would be no reason for me to call or go over there. It will probably be a minute before they even find her. I'll just let it play out."

Misty sat for a minute trying to determine Chris's sincerity about leaving the game. "Papi, you've never broken a promise to me. Don't start now."

CHAPTER 22

Three weeks had passed since Val's murder. Chris watched the news every night and still no story had broken. Chris had five kilos remaining, and he was out the game for good. Benny already promised Chris that he would get them when he returned home from a wedding he was attending in Chicago.

Chris was sitting in the Blue Note sipping his Hennessy when Manny came in behind him. "What's going on, playa?" Manny asked.

"Just chillin'," Chris replied as he stood. The two men shook hands.

"Yo, what's going on with Benny? I've been trying to get with him since yesterday. He ain't answer."

"He's out of town. Why? What's up?"

"Shit . . . you know. I'm trying to get on."

Chris just looked at the brother.

"I need to grab five of them joints. I'm all done and I'm missin' loot."

Chris knew Benny wanted the last five for himself and wasn't planning on cutting no deals. He didn't want to leave Manny out in the cold though.

"Ain't really nothing crackin'. I might be able to get you a half chicken. Something to hold you over until he gets back," Chris said.

"Damn. You can't get me five? I really need them," Manny said, almost begging.

"Benny got everything. You want the half or not, fam'?"

Manny thought for a minute and finally spoke. "If that's all I can get, I can't complain."

"Cool. Give me a few, and I'll hit your phone."

"Okay fam', but try to hurry." Manny got up and left.

Chris finished his drink and followed him. He didn't really want to break one of the kilos down, but he had given Benny his word. Benny wouldn't mind the half kilo and would probably have given it to Manny anyway.

The drive to the storage unit and back took about an hour and fifteen minutes. Chris dialed Manny's number and he answered immediately.

"What's good?" Manny asked.

"Andro's in fifteen minutes," Chris replied.

"Okay. What's the damage?"

"Just bring me ten bucks," Chris said, referencing ten thousand dollars.

When Manny arrived, Chris was shooting pool. Chris pointed to a bag sitting on the chair and said, "That's you."

Manny passed Chris a Crown Royal bag with the money inside. Business was complete, so the two men embraced as Manny turned and headed out the door. His stomach knotted. He had just violated a major rule of the game and sold Chris out. At first, he convinced himself that Chris deserved it for shooting him. Now that the deed had been done, Manny found it hard to even look at himself in the rearview mirror as he watched two DEA agents in the backseat talking to their supervisor.

When he got busted, his plan was to get Benny. Getting Chris wasn't a thought out plan, and he regretted it more and more with the passing seconds. Being that Chris was from McKeesport, he wanted to avoid bringing him down. Telling was bad enough, but telling on someone from the hood put his whole family at risk. Chris was one of them people that everyone loved. Now Manny would have to testify in front of a grand jury concerning Chris's small empire. In exchange, he wouldn't be charged with the gun and drugs he had been caught with during a traffic stop a few months back. There were no offers to relocate him and his family. The Feds really didn't care. They would use him up and throw him back to the wolves. Manny had promised them five kilos. Now that he only provided them with enough evidence to indict Chris on a half kilo, he was lucky to still be going free on his charge.

After Manny left, Chris finished shooting pool and headed out the door. On the drive home, he reflected on his life and everything he had been through. He felt like the luckiest man in the world to be alive and free. He had a beautiful wife and daughter and enough money to live comfortably for a long time to come.

CHAPTER 23

Six months had passed since Chris had left the game alone. There was still no news of Val's death, which made Chris uneasy, but he would cross that bridge when he came to it. After Benny purchased the last of the cocaine, Chris never looked back. With help from Trent, the bartender at Hitches, Chris opened his first business. It was a small detail shop called "Crazy Clean." He wasn't making millions of dollars. However, he was happy. He was at the shop all day and went home to his family at night. Learning the ins and outs of the business fueled Chris's drive to succeed. The more he learned, the better the business became. What started off as a few hundred dollars per week blossomed into $1,000 per week within months. Chris was proud. People would always tell Chris how smart he was. How if he applied as much effort into a legitimate business as he did to the streets, he could do anything. Initially, he never believed them, but now their words crystallized and he never felt better. Chris realized that all the money he had couldn't make him as content. What really made him happy was his family and his success as a businessman.

The day was March 1, and Chris was at the shop early preparing for his March Madness promotion. All his services were half off, and his phone had been ringing off the hook with appointments. Because of the increase in business, Chris hired two employees, which excited him. His ability to hire people proved that he was growing and doing something positive for his community, which was something he was becoming more familiar with. He supported all the local little league teams by buying the kids uniforms and tennis shoes. Chris also donated to the YMCA and sponsored camping trips for the kids. He held a fundraiser for the March of Dimes. He also spent time at the Literacy Council teaching people to read. For him it was about helping people. It did good for his soul. He knew one day he would have to answer to God, so he was trying to balance the scales in his favor. He had done wrong for so many years. Too consumed with his thoughts concerning the changes he had made, Chris didn't see them coming till they were filing in through the doors.

Clad in black uniforms with full swat gear, the agents surrounded him in seconds with weapons drawn, ready to fire at the first sign of resistance.

"FBI! Let me see your hands! Get 'em up! Get on the ground!" they yelled.

Chris was dizzy from the shock. He couldn't figure out what was going on. The six months he had spent legit seemed like a lifetime. He was arrested without incident and taken to the post office in downtown Pittsburgh, which shared the building with the Federal Courthouse.

An officer led him into a cell that looked and smelled of disinfectant. The cleanliness amazed him. The intake process at the county jail was trifling. He felt like he was waiting to see a doctor, not a judge.

After waiting a few hours, a guard escorted Chris into a courtroom where his indictment was read. The judge remanded him to jail, and his arraignment was scheduled for the following day.

THE DEVIL'S GAME

After being transported to the county jail, Chris began the intake process. He made it to his classification unit also known as the SHU. He immediately crawled into his bunk, exhausted. Staring at the ceiling, Chris replayed the events of the day over and over. He was relieved to know that Misty and his daughter had been unaffected. The Feds never went to his home. He was even more relieved that none of his storage units had been searched. Therefore, he wasn't taking an enormous financial hit. The origin of his arrest related directly to his indictment. Title 18 §841(b). Possession with intent to distribute more than 500, but less than 1,000 grams of cocaine.

"Manny," Chris said aloud when he read the indictment. Chris hadn't sold anything less than five kilos at a time for over a year and a half. That is except for the half kilo he gave Manny.

The time was nothing. Misty had spoken to the lawyer. It was too early to tell exactly, but Chris was looking at a five-year mandatory minimum with a few enhancements for his prior offenses, so it was nothing too serious. Chris could accept that. He was two months short of twenty-one. When he got out he would have his whole life ahead of him.

Manny crossing him was something he wasn't willing to accept. Chris had promised Misty he was going to leave the game alone. That promise would have to be broken. Manny was going to die. His treason would not go unpunished.

The following day, Chris's arraignment was short and simple. He was denied bail. The US Attorney was able to convince the magistrate judge that Chris was a threat to the community. Manny made sure of it. He assured the government that his life was in danger and that if freed, Chris would surely seek retribution. Chris prayed Manny hadn't mentioned Quick's murder. In reality, he didn't know the details behind Quick's murder. He was still listed as a missing person. Plus Manny would have to implicate himself.

The night after Chris was arraigned he was moved to general population. He put in a visiting list. The only people he was interested in seeing was Misty and Benny. Misty argued that Autumn needed to see her daddy, but Chris refused.

"Don't you ever bring my daughter down here," he warned her.

A few days passed before his list cleared. Misty had been upset that Chris had requested to see Benny first.

"Papi, what you mean let Benny come? I'm your wife. I need to see you," she complained.

"Mama, I need to holla at him. You know I want to see you, but it's important that I see him."

"Christopher, don't be into no stupid shit." He cut her off.

"Kill all that talk on this phone. I'll see you Wednesday. I love you, and you're gonna have to trust me," he said firmly.

A few hours after Chris hung up with Misty, he was called for a visit. When he stepped in front of the small window and saw Benny, Chris couldn't help but notice his friend was uneasy.

"You all right, fam'?" Chris asked.

"I hate jails. I can't even believe I'm down this motherfucker. I must really love you, lil' nigga. So what's up? You cool?" he asked.

"Yeah. But this shit's crazy. Remember that last joint I gave you? How I took that piece out for Manny?"

Benny just nodded.

"That pussy set me up. If you hadn't gone to that wedding, this visit would be the other way around."

Benny stared at his friend through the glass unsure of what to say. Chris continued without waiting for a response. "I want that motherfucker's head."

"Yo fam', we're on these phones. You need to chill," Benny said.

Chris stared at his friend like he was stupid. "How they recording something and the wire goes straight from your phone to mine. Quit with the bullshit."

Benny wasn't about any violence. When Richey smacked his sister up, Benny asked to go along with them out of pure emotion. He wasn't trying to catch a body. He wasn't a chump and would do what he had to do to protect himself or his loved ones, but cold-blooded murder was different. He was stuck between a rock and a hard place. Participate in Manny's death or most likely become Chris's enemy.

Chris sensed his apprehension, so he spoke up to ease his friend's mind. "You don't have to kill nobody. I just need you to holler at the young boy, Jihad," Chris said.

"And say what?" Benny asked.

"Fifty thousand for Manny's head."

Relieved that he wasn't being asked to murder anyone, Benny nodded. "I got you."

After business was out the way, the two men spent the rest of the hour speaking about Chris's situation. Benny left with promises to hold Chris down.

"Hold me down by doing what I asked. That's all I want from you, fam'," Chris responded.

Doing time in Allegheny County blew by. Misty visited Chris twice a week. For the most part Chris avoided people, choosing his acquaintances wisely. He stayed away from cards, television, and any sports. He wasn't about to put himself through no drama over some bullshit.

Chris had been down almost three months when the news reached him about Manny's death. His decapitated body was left on his mother's doorstep. His head was never found.

Homicide had come to question Chris, but he only requested his lawyer, which left them at a dead end.

CHAPTER 24

While Chris was in jail, Jihad, Crook, Teku and Tree blew up. They had McKeesport on lock and formed a small clique called Point Blank Mob. Their following grew like a virus, and before long nothing happened in the hood without their knowledge. Chris's kindness toward them was not forgotten. So when the word came down that Manny's head was on the chopping block they didn't even care about the money.

Manny had sought refuge at his cousin Lisa's house. He had been staying in her basement and not venturing out much, hoping that eventually people would forget about him. He had enough money saved up that he didn't have to worry about hustling. He could lay low for years if necessary. It was Lisa who ended up sealing his fate.

She had slipped up and mentioned Manny to Teku and Tree's sister, Love, one night at the bar. Complaining about Manny lying and thinking that because he paid all her bills he didn't have to do shit. Lisa never considered that Love would run back and tell her brothers, or that her brothers were in any way connected to Chris.

Lisa was at work when Jihad and Crook made their move. The two men kicked in the basement door and caught an unsuspecting Manny sitting on the couch in his boxers watching a movie.

"What the fuck?" Manny hollered as he reached for his firearm.

He was too late. Crook's gun exploded and sent Manny crashing into the wall. Crook turned to walk out when Jihad hollered after him, "Dog, where you going?"

"Home nigga, he's dead. What the fuck you want me to do?"

"Benny said Chris wants this punk's head," Jihad said as if Crook should understand.

"Fool, it was a figure of speech. We killed the nigga, now let's go," Crook said.

Jihad didn't listen. Instead, he removed a knife from his pocket and positioned himself over Manny and prepared to cut.

"Yo dog, somebody might of heard that gunshot. I ain't gonna sit here while you try to cut a nigga's head off. Especially with that," Crook said in disbelief.

"What's wrong with my knife?" Jihad asked.

"Nigga, it's a steak knife."

"Dog, this ain't no steak knife. This some Cutco shit. Bought this shit for my mom. Joint cuts thru anything. They even had a pair of scissors that cut through a penny," Jihad said proudly.

Crook realized that he couldn't get through to Jihad, so he grabbed a blanket off Manny's bed and said, "Here, wrap that punk up in here and we'll take him with us. But if we get caught I'm gonna be pissed."

Jihad responded by dragging Manny on top of the blanket and they proceeded to wrap him up. Crook, being the bigger of the two, hoisted Manny up onto his shoulder and they left the house. They put Manny in the trunk of the stolen car for this occasion.

"So now what?" Crook asked.

"We'll take this fool to the garage on Ridge Street," Jihad said.

"And do what?"

"Dog, I'm cutting this pussy's head off. Then I don't care. We can drop him off at his mama's house," Jihad said, liking the sound of his idea.

Crook just shook his head in bewilderment. Jihad was always taking things to the extreme. Usually Crook could control his friend, but when he had his mind set on something he ran with it, and there was no stopping until he crossed the finish line.

They arrived at the garage and drove inside. Jihad and Crook purchased garages to keep various things inside that were better not kept in their homes. They got out the car and opened the trunk. Crook tried to watch but almost threw up at the sight of Jihad cutting savagely into Manny's flesh.

"Dog, hurry the fuck up with that shit," Crook said, becoming sick.

"Fuck! This pussy got tough skin," he said, laughing.

The brutality lasted for five minutes before Jihad finally popped up from the trunk brandishing his trophy. "I told you this shit cuts through anything." He grabbed a garbage bag off the shelf and deposited the head in it. Afterwards, the two men drove Manny to his mother's house and made sure nobody was watching as they hoisted his body out of the trunk and deposited it next to his mother's door and left.

The next day, Jihad called Benny and asked him to meet him. Benny agreed. He drove to McKeesport and picked Jihad up. Jihad jumped in Benny's truck with a bag. Benny eyed it suspiciously and then asked, "What's up? What's in the bag?"

"That thing you asked for," Jihad replied.

"What thing?" Benny asked.

Without answering, Jihad unzipped the duffel bag. Benny looked in and almost vomited. "Nigga, what the fuck is that?"

"It's Manny's head. Y'all said y'all wanted his head."

"Yo, it was a figure of speech." Benny frowned, amazed that someone took him so literally.

"That's what Crook said, too, but I wanted to make sure." Jihad was a little irritated that Crook had been right.

"Yo, get that shit out of my car. I'll get that paper for you and bring it down tomorrow."

"Don't worry about it. Tell Chris that shit was on the house." Jihad got out the car and walked away.

Benny realized it was Tuesday and that Chris could get visits, so he called Misty to make sure it was okay for him to go visit. She told him it was and he headed straight to the county jail.

He waited almost two hours to see Chris, but when he got up there he was still agitated from the meeting with Jihad. When Chris lifted the phone, Benny said, "Yo, let me tell you what these nut ass niggaz just did." Benny shook his head, looked down at the floor and back up at Chris. He rubbed his hand over his face once and shook his head again.

His gestures baffled Chris. "What's up, fam'? You okay?"

"Hell no! Fucking Jihad called me and wanted to see me. So I ride down to check his little ass out. He gets in my truck with a fucking bag."

"And. So what?" Chris replied.

"Nigga, this fool had Manny's head in it!"

An astonished Chris couldn't help but let out a quick laugh. "Are you fucking serious?" Chris was impressed.

"Nigga, you act like that shit don't bother you. Fool, this nigga got in my truck with someone's head."

"That's good. That means the young boy knows how to follow instructions. I like that shit. I'll make sure you get that fifty stacks by the end of the day."

"Yo, he said he don't want it. He did that shit for free," Benny replied.

Chris just stared at his man. *Damn, that young boy was thorough. Country sure knew how to pick them.* He had to find a way to repay the young boy for his loyalty. Dudes like that came along once in a blue moon. One thing was for sure, with Manny out of the way Chris would sleep better at night. Now he could do his time and come home without any loose ends.

CHAPTER 25

It took almost eleven months to go through the formalities of all Chris's legal proceedings. Finally, he was sentenced on February 7, 2001, to eighty-four months. He was given credit for the time he had served in the county. Also, he would be given fifty-four good days per year provided he stay out of trouble and do his time. Chris could even get twelve months off for good behavior if he participated in the drug program. But from what he heard he might not be eligible because of the gun charges on his record. He wouldn't find out until he got to his designated prison. Regardless, as long as everything went right he would be released sometime in 2006. His lawyer also requested that he be sent to FCI Beckley, which was located in Beaver, West Virginia. Jesus was there, so it would make Chris's bid a lot smoother being with his man. It would also give him the opportunity to come clean and rid himself of the guilt he was harboring.

A few weeks after sentencing, Chris was transported from the Allegheny County Jail to Pittsburgh International Airport. When he arrived, the scene from the movie *Con Air* immediately came to mind. The van he rode in pulled up to the huge 747 that was surrounded by US Marshals in bulletproof vests brandishing AR-15's and shot guns.

Are they serious? Chris thought. The marshals' precautions were an overkill.

THE DEVIL'S GAME

When Chris first received his indictment, the whole thing seemed a bit much. It read, "The United States of America vs. Christopher Michaels." It wasn't like he was a terrorist. It was as if he pissed the whole damn country off, and they were seeking retribution for his actions.

Once loaded on the plane, Chris's feet were shackled to the floor and his seat belt was fastened. Looking out the window, the reality of his situation really set in. *Damn, I fucked up.* Then his attention was diverted to a section of the plane's wing that had a piece of duct tape on it.

"Is that duct tape?" Chris asked the man sitting next to him.

"Welcome to the Feds, young blood," said the old head with a laugh.

Chris didn't find it funny, but kept his worries to himself. He couldn't complain. He didn't know much about prison. What he did know was that they didn't give a fuck about you or your complaints. He was now the property of the Bureau of Prisons. A slave according to the Thirteenth Amendment of the Constitution of these United States, which declares: "Neither slavery nor involuntary servitude, except as punishment for crime where party shall have been duly convicted, shall exist within the United States, or any place subject to their jurisdiction." In short, Chris was fucked.

So instead of complaining, Chris closed his eyes and drifted off. He awoke to the plane's descent and thanked God for a safe flight. One by one the prisoners had their feet unshackled, and they exited the plane through a long corridor. Chris was surprised to learn that he wasn't in an airport. Instead, Chris walked out of the passageway and straight into FTC Oklahoma. The Federal Transfer Center was basically a temporary holding facility that housed inmates until they were sent off to their designated prisons. Jesus had once told Chris that federal prisons were the major leagues of the penal system. He wasn't lying.

The classification process took up the rest of the day. During this time, Chris learned that the judge's recommendation was successful, and he was headed to FCI Beckley.

He was finally loaded onto an elevator along with a few other inmates and taken upstairs to his unit. Everybody was locked in when they got there. Chris was taken directly to his cell and went to sleep.

A few hours later, someone rustled Chris from his sleep and told him that he was leaving. This surprised him. While downstairs, other inmates whom had been through FTC Oklahoma before said they waited months to leave. Chris was on his way to his prison in just a few hours. This was a blessing because it allowed him to get settled and start doing his time.

An hour and a half later, Chris was in the air. Their first stop was an airport in Kentucky where a group of inmates were unloaded en route to their designated prison, and a new group was brought aboard the aircraft en route to theirs.

Chris's stop was next. They landed in Lewisburg, West Virginia, where he and a few other inmates were taken off the aircraft, loaded into a waiting van, and shuttled to the prison.

By the time they arrived at the prison, it was almost two in the afternoon. The tedious intake process lasted over three hours, but by 6 p.m. Chris was walking across the compound en route to the A&O unit. When he walked into the unit, heads snapped to attention as other inmates looked to see who the new guys were and whether or not they knew them.

Chris looked around also, but there were no familiar faces. The guard directed Chris to his cell, and with that, his time in prison began. He walked into the small room, surprised to see that it wasn't half bad. A nice, thick mattress was a welcomed sight. After eleven months in the county, it looked more like a pillow top than a lump of polyester filling.

Chris was getting settled when a brother knocked on his door and said, "Yo, you Chris?"

"Yep, what's up?" Chris asked.

"Somebody is out front looking for you," said the brother.

Chris thanked him and the man turned to leave. Chris knew who was looking for him. He didn't know many people in the Feds, so he walked outside to a smiling Jesus.

"Good to see you," Jesus said as he hugged Chris tightly.

"Same here," Chris replied as he returned the embrace.

"Here goes some stuff that will make you comfortable." Jesus pointed to a huge bag sitting next to him on the ground.

"How did you know I was here?" Chris asked.

"I know everything." Jesus laughed. "I got a guy that helps out in your unit. I asked him to look out for your name on the new loads. He let me know at lunch that you were on your way. I got you some boots, sweats, T-shirts, and a shit load of food. You should be good for a few weeks."

"Yo, I appreciate that. So what now?" Chris asked, hoping to gather some advice.

"I live in that unit, Pine A upper. There is one more move at 7:30. Come out and we'll go to the yard for an hour, and I'll break everything down to you."

"Cool," Chris said.

"The compound is now closed. The move is over," the voice sounded out over the PA system.

"That's the end of the move, my friend. I will see you in an hour," Jesus said.

The two men touched fists and then went their separate ways.

Once back in his cell, Chris began to unload his bag and smiled at Jesus's generosity. Jesus had truly taken care of him. He had a little bit of everything, which would make his transition a lot easier.

At 7:30, Chris heard them call a one-way move to the units and went outside. Jesus was waiting for him and explained that there was a five-minute move to the units, and then another five-minute move to recreation. When the move to recreation was called, the two men walked silently across the compound and were forced to go through a metal detector. Once on the other side they headed to the track.

"So you all right, my friend?" asked Jesus.

"Yeah, I'm good. Just trying to get this shit over with," Chris responded.

"I feel you. Your time will be over soon. Misty said they gave you eighty-four months."

"Yeah, over that snake ass Manny."

Jesus laughed. "You got it all wrong, my friend. You are in prison because of Chris, not Manny. Chris was the one who sold Manny drugs. Chris was the one who let Manny close to him."

Chris just sat there silently and digested Jesus's words. He always seized an opportunity to educate Chris, and Chris always listened. What Jesus was saying was all true. Chris should have got out the game a long time ago. Now he was in prison trying to hold on to his family and everything he had worked so hard for.

"So how are you holding up?" Chris asked Jesus.

"I'm good, my friend. For me, this is home for twenty-years. But I'm okay. It was hard when I heard Valerie was killed. Her father sent me a letter saying they found her body. They went down there when they hadn't heard from her for a week. I hated being in here. There was nothing I could do. But I am good now."

Chris instantly became nervous at the mention of Val's name. Until now, he knew nothing about what happened when he left her. Nothing on the news. No repercussions. It was as if it had never happened.

"Jesus,   about   Val—"
Jesus cut him off, "I don't want to know, Chris . . . please, it's better that I don't know."

Chris just sat there bewildered, looking at Jesus trying to understand. Chris intended to come clean to tell Jesus the truth about the woman he loved. Jesus noticed the confused look on Chris's face. "Chris, all I got in here is memories. In here I found out that Valerie wasn't the woman I thought she was. I know that whatever happened she probably deserved it. But it is easier for me to remember the woman I loved. So my friend, please just let me have my memories."

They walked a few laps in silence before Chris finally spoke. "So what do I do now, Jesus? What happens next?"

"Time . . . and make the best of it. There are a lot of programs in education. Other than that just stay out the way and do what you have to, to go home. It's not hard," Jesus said.

The men continued to walk until they recalled everyone to the units for count. Once they arrived in front of their unit, the two men embraced one more time and went inside.

CHAPTER 26

Chris adapted well to prison. He had been at Beckley almost a year. He had enrolled in GED classes and had a job in recreation. Working in recreation didn't pay a lot, but it allowed him the opportunity to work out. Jesus also worked in recreation, so the two men spent a lot of time together.

They rarely spoke about the streets, but today was different.

"So what you gonna do when you go home?" Jesus asked.

"I don't know. That's a long time away. Why you ask?" Chris replied.

"I'm just wondering if you plan on leaving the game alone."

"I think about it all the time. I tell myself yes, but it seems like every time I walk away something pulls me back in. I mean, I got plenty of money now, but I won't be going home for another four and a half years. Anything can happen. I know Misty is tired already."

"Misty loves you. Don't worry yourself about mi prima. She will be there," Jesus said sternly.

"I know she'll be there, but it might not be the same. Honestly, Jesus, the only reason I ever wanted to leave the streets was because of my family. If I lose them, the streets are all I have."

"You got your whole life ahead of you. Do you want to spend it here? These people gave me twenty years, my friend. They don't care about us. People rape children and get less time than drug offenders. Don't allow yourself to be their victim. I love you like my blood, so please listen to me."

Chris let Jesus's words sink in, but it was still too early for him to commit to a certain way of life upon his release. The truth was, Chris didn't know what he wanted when he got out. It seemed like every time he did the right thing something bad happened and he had to start all over. The only thing he was truly successful at was the streets. He had opened his own business only to have it stripped away. The streets just didn't want to let go of him.

Chris knew that when he went home, the streets would be waiting. Jihad and Crook were out there getting major money. Misty kept Chris informed about their activities every time she visited. They were buying up properties left and right. They even had a news story concerning their clique, The Point Blank Mob.

Overnight the crew turned into an army. They were a target, but Jihad and Crook were smart. They would separate themselves from all the soldiers on the street catching any kind of heat.

Jihad would stop by Misty's mother's home every now and then and drop money off. Even though Chris didn't need it, he still appreciated the gesture. Nobody, including Benny, ever did anything for Chris. If it wasn't for Misty he would be alone. It was just like Jesus had told him one day: "Out of sight, out of mind."

As the months continued to roll by, Chris became more and more comfortable. He began to care less about the streets. He no longer had dreams about home. He dreamed about the people around him. They had become his family and friends. Instead of dreaming about being in the club with Country, he shot pool in the recreation yard with Jesus.

Misty continued to stay strong. He could tell she was tired, but she never complained. She made the trip to Beckley every month. A lot of brothers didn't ever see the visiting room, or the "dance floor," as everyone liked to call it. So Chris was grateful for Misty's loyalty. He had finally broke down and allowed her to bring Autumn. His daughter was huge. The first time he saw her in there she was two and a half years old. He couldn't believe how much she had grown. The pictures didn't do her justice. He cried like a baby while he rocked her in his arms. At that moment Chris knew he would never hustle again.

Chris graduated from his GED class and was immediately put into the college program. He wouldn't be able to get his degree in prison unless he helped pay. That privilege had been revoked from prisoners. Citizens were complaining that it wasn't fair for convicted felons to receive a free education when people who abided by the laws had to pay. Chris didn't see any point in this philosophy. He felt that if you gave a person the opportunity to do things the right way, then they would have a better chance of leading a legitimate life. Chris later realized that prison was a business. The government warehoused prisoners like merchandise. Prisoners created jobs, which in turn boosted the economy while making the politicians look like they were tough on crime. The truth is, 70% of federal prisoners are non-violent drug offenders. So instead of allowing Chris to complete his degree, they gave him all the credits he would need except three. To receive his degree, he would have to enroll in a correspondence course to complete his associate's degree. It was a $400 investment, but when Chris finally finished he felt amazing.

THE DEVIL'S GAME

They had a graduation ceremony in the visiting room. Misty, Autumn, and Beverly came. Chris's mother also came, and when he saw her, his heart fell into his stomach. He hadn't seen her in years. She never approved of his lifestyle, so they fell apart. Chris would try to give her money, but she would never accept it. She remarried, and she and Gary sought refuge in their own little world. Chris was content not to be any part of it.

Now seeing his mother walk across the visiting room, he opened his arms to her and she fell into his grip.

"I love you, Christopher," his mom said, crying uncontrollably. She hadn't been this proud of her son since he was a child. All he had brought her was pain. He had been a reflection of her failure as a mother. Now he stood in front of her a college graduate.

Misty and her mother looked on with smiles. Autumn jumped out of Misty's arms and ran to join the hug. Nobody hugged her daddy except her.

CHAPTER 27

Chris's time was getting short. He was counting down the months and all he could think about were his plans upon release. Misty had graduated and was teaching third grade at Monongahela Elementary School, which was the same school Autumn attended. Chris was devastated to miss her first day of school, but Misty had taken pictures of the whole event and mailed them to him.

Chris intended to re-open his detail shop. He realized that losing his detail shop wasn't due to his lack of business etiquette. He had lost it because of mistakes he had made in the past. Now with a business degree, Chris knew how to handle the situation a lot better and was excited to give it another try.

Chris had let go of the streets completely. In his mind, hustling wasn't even an option. However, two months short of Chris's release, his name was announced at mail call and his life had changed forever.

The letter was a simple piece of mail to anyone but Chris. However, when he saw the return address his knee's got weak. He nervously opened the letter as he walked to his cell. Inside the letter was a picture of Autumn playing outside their home. The name on the outside of the envelope was none other than Val's.

THE DEVIL'S GAME

What the fuck? Chris thought. He knew for a fact that Val was dead.

Chris was baffled. Scared. He knew what the picture of Autumn implied. His daughter had become a target. Whoever sent it knew he had killed Val. Whoever sent it wanted Chris to feel helpless. What could a man in prison do to protect his family? Not a damn thing.

He needed to talk to Misty, but it was the end of the month and he was out of minutes. Prisoners were only given three hundred minutes per month, and once they were gone it was over. The alternative was to have Jesus call home and warn Misty. Chris sat patiently and waited for the recreation move before dinner. When the move was called, Chris ran over to Jesus's unit and hollered out for him. Jesus came to the door and stepped outside.

"Que pasa. You look like shit," Jesus said, noticing that Chris wasn't himself.

"Jesus, I need you to call Misty and tell her to get Autumn somewhere safe. They have to leave the house."

"What are you talking about?" Jesus asked.

"Jesus please. I'm out of minutes. I'll explain later. Just please do this for me."

"Of course. Just meet me when they call your unit for dinner. We eat first. We'll go to rec."

"Thank you," Chris said as he turned and walked away. He was a nervous wreck. Why wait this long? Val had been dead over six years. Was this somebody's idea of a joke?

Chris's unit was called for chow and he met Jesus outside. The two men walked to recreation and found an empty bench on the softball field.

"What's good, my friend?"

Without answering, Chris passed Jesus the letter he had received. Seeing Val's name made Jesus instantly suspicious.

"What is this?" Jesus asked.

"It's a picture of my daughter," replied Chris.

"Why does it have my wife's name on it?"

Chris was without options. The only choice he had was to tell Jesus everything about Val's death. He started at the beginning and explained everything except Rico's murder. He told him of Val's advances and how the two had eventually slept together. He explained her inability to understand that Chris didn't want anything to do with her. Finally, Chris came to the part about her admission of putting Jesus behind bars and his own reaction.

"Jesus, I killed your wife. Everything happened so fast . . . I'm sorry," Chris said with tears in his eyes. He could see that Jesus was in pain.

"I really don't know what to say, my friend," Jesus replied somberly. He had suspected Chris of the murder. Val didn't know many people in Pittsburgh and made it a point to keep to herself. Chris would have been the only person capable of having a motive to kill her. He was the only person she conducted business with. Jesus loved his wife dearly. Deep down he knew that she had been the one to set him up, but he never said anything. He knew that she was a snake, but he tried to change her. He believed that one day she would be comfortable enough with him to put down her guards. Therefore, he didn't blame anyone but himself for her setting him up.

Chris just sat and stared at his friend, his father figure. He owed everything to this man, and he repaid him by sleeping with, and then killing his wife.

"Chris, have you ever met Val's family? Do you know who they are?" Jesus asked.

"Never," Chris replied.

Jesus just shook his head at Chris's naivety. "You really don't know what you did by killing Valerie. Valerie is the granddaughter of a man named Nicholai Storsky."

"So, who is that?" Chris asked.

"The devil. He is a lieutenant in the Russian mafia. This man will stop at nothing to see you suffer if he knows you killed his granddaughter."

"But six years. Why wait six years?"

"That's simple. He wanted you to get to know your daughter. To create a bond with her as he created one with his granddaughter. He knows that you are in prison and that you ain't going anywhere. Now that you are coming home, he's ready," Jesus said.

"For what?" Chris asked.

"Retribution. You're now at war with the Russian mafia."

"Jesus, what am I going to do?"

"You are on your own." Jesus got up from the bleachers and walked away without looking back.

CHAPTER 28

Chris's release day came and the only thing Chris was concerned about was the safety of Misty and their child. Misty was at the door waiting for him wearing a bright yellow summer dress with some Jimmy Choo pumps. Chris couldn't wait to be inside her. It felt great to be free. So far, Autumn was safe. Misty, at Chris's insistence, gave Autumn to her mother to watch. Chris knew he had to deal with Nicholai. Men like him didn't walk away. However, Chris didn't have any soldiers to go to war.

Jihad and Crook had been killed, and their whole crew had been locked away three years into his prison sentence. They had died in a gunfight with the police. From what Chris was told, Jihad and Crook were on the run and had left the state. Jihad found out that he left behind a son and came back to McKeesport to see him. Somebody tipped off the police and when they attempted to arrest the duo, Jihad and Crook chose to hold court in the street. They were on the run for the murder of an undercover DEA agent, so they were left without a choice.

Benny was still out there, but he wasn't trying to do anything. Chris had only talked to him a few times during his whole sentence. After the murder of Manny, Benny started acting funny and keeping his distance.

"So what are you going to do, Chris?" Misty asked, bringing him out of his thoughts as they drove away from the prison.

"About what?" Chris asked.

"Whatever it is that's going on. Are you even going to tell me why our daughter is hiding? I had to enroll our daughter in private school. You have my mother scared to death. Christopher, what is going on?"

Misty had a right to know, so Chris began to explain. "No! No! You told me they wouldn't know. Please God. . . . what does this have to do with our daughter?" she pleaded.

"Maybe nothing. Maybe everything. I don't know, mama. All I know is that I will die before I let anything happen to her. I just got to work on getting a team together, so I can go at these boys," Chris said.

Misty pulled to the side of the road, unable to drive. "What do you mean 'get a team together'? You just did seven years, you fool. I did seven years with you. Do you want to go back?"

"If I have to, then so be it. I won't let nothing happen to our daughter."

Misty pulled the car back on the highway and didn't say anything. She couldn't believe what Chris was saying. She had waited seven years for her husband, and what for? He was coming home and jumping right back into the streets that had taken him away from her. She now realized that no matter what, there would always be a reason for him. Normal people would have turned the issue over to the police. Normal people wouldn't be in this situation. Chris wasn't normal. He lived in the streets and by its rules. In his world, he solved problems with violence. In his world, he ran over anything in his way to

succeed. It was time for her to let go. The streets could have
him.

They drove to Misty's mother's house, and Chris ran inside
to his daughter. She was about to be six-years old.
Surprisingly, he felt like he had never missed a single day. He
spent the next hour with her before Misty drove him to the
halfway house. He didn't even try to approach his wife for
sex. He could tell by her demeanor that she was mad. Chris
understood his wife's frustrations.

He was required to stay at the Renewal Center for a six-
month period. As long as he did everything he was supposed
to do, he would be on home confinement within sixty days.

During the trip downtown, Misty finally spoke,
"Christopher, I can't do this no more."

Chris didn't say anything. He knew it was coming.

"Aren't you going to say anything? Do you even fucking
care!" Misty hollered.

"Mama, I love you more than you could ever imagine. But
I don't know what you want from me? What am I supposed to
do?" Chris asked.

"You're supposed to walk away from this game. To
appreciate your family and want to be with them. But you are
always finding excuses to go back. When is it enough? You're
a millionaire. You have everything you want. But it still ain't
enough," Misty said, beginning to cry.

"Do you think I like jail? Do you think I like being away
from you and my daughter? That shit eats me up. These
people are not playing, Misty. They want me dead, and
possibly Autumn. I don't have no other choice."

THE DEVIL'S GAME

"We could leave. Whenever you get out of the halfway house let's just get out of here. Leave all this behind. We can go anywhere."

"I can't run. They will find us. I have to deal with this. I started it, so I have to finish it."

With those words, nothing else was said. Misty pulled in front of the halfway house. Chris grabbed his bag out of the backseat and got out. Misty watched as he walked inside the building and said softly, "I love you, baby."

Inside the halfway house, Chris was an emotional wreck. He went through his orientation without hearing a single word. By the time he got upstairs to the seventh floor he was drained. He crawled onto his bunk and drifted off.

The next morning he awoke and went into his counselor's office where he had to go over more rules and regulations. She gave him a pass to go shopping and pick up some necessities. The following day he was permitted to go look for work.

Misty had calmed down and decided to stick by her husband. She had come this far, so the extra mile wouldn't kill her. She picked him up a block from the halfway house and they proceeded to McKeesport. Misty's mother still owned Rico's construction company. Chris had to meet the supervisor and fill out some paperwork. The halfway house was unaware that Chris had a job lined up, so he had the whole day to search for a job. After filling out the paperwork, Chris and Misty would have the remainder of the day to catch up.

They went to the Best Western on Lebanon Church Road and got a room. When they walked through the door, Chris eased up behind his wife and put his arms around her. It felt like heaven to have her in his arms. He felt like the protector again. Misty melted into his grip as he placed small kisses across the back of her neck. He took her ear lobe between his moist lips and whispered, "I love you, mama." She felt the pressure of his manhood against her lower back. She turned in his arms and began to undress him. Chris was under the impression that his first sexual experience after being gone for so long would be over quickly, but he was mistaken. The couple made love for almost an hour before he climaxed. When the eruption came, Chris's body went weak and he collapsed on his wife in what felt like eternal bliss. Afterward, the couple lay on the bed holding one another until it was time to go.

Chris's time in the halfway house was uneventful. He continued working for Misty's mother while on home confinement and upon his release. Autumn remained in private school, but now lived at home with Misty and Chris. Chris would drive her to and from school every day since he was working in McKeesport. He was in the process of opening his detail shop, but had yet to find the perfect place. Until then, he was content and his probation officer stayed off his back.

Although the issue with Val's family was not forgotten, Chris relaxed somewhat as time went on. Then one day Autumn came in from playing outside and handed Chris a letter. "Daddy look!" Autumn's ringlets fell down in her face as she held up a piece of paper. Chris took the paper from her hand. "Welcome home" it read in blood. All the color drained from his face.

Chris jumped to his feet. "Autumn, who gave you this?"

"Some man," said his daughter, whose voice wavered, obviously scared by her daddy's reaction.

"Baby, what did the man look like? Please tell daddy."

"I don't know, Daddy." Autumn started to cry.

Chris realized he was scaring her, so he immediately swooped her up in his arms trying to console her. Misty came in the room hearing all of the commotion. "What's going on?" she asked.

Chris handed her the letter and she began to cry as she ripped the letter up and threw it to the ground.

"What are we going to do?" she asked.

"The only thing I know how," Chris replied as he handed his daughter to Misty and headed for the door.

Misty knew that she couldn't stop him. She didn't want to. Chris was trying to do the right thing, but they wouldn't let him. So she would now support her husband and if need be, die with him. He was trying to protect Autumn, and that was the most important thing to Misty.

CHAPTER 29

Chris had been out of the game so long that everything had changed. When he first got home, a young boy jumped out of a Cadillac truck and walked up to him and gave him five-hundred bucks. It took Chris a minute to realize that the young man before him was a small boy when he left. The boy had said, "Welcome home, OG. You was always there for me when I was a kid. I want to make sure you cool."

Chris didn't need the money, but it was nice to have people in the hood pay homage to him.

With that said, Chris's greatest obstacle would be finding thorough brothers who would be willing to go to war at all cost. Chris had enough money to get started, but the only way to continue keeping people happy would be to establish a connection and open the drug game back up. He may have been a millionaire, but money would only last so long. A war would cost money, and Chris wasn't trying to go broke fighting it. His first stop was Benny.

Benny hadn't changed much. He was still doing what he was doing when Chris left. Benny didn't have aspirations to be a drug kingpin of any sort. He was content with getting by, so he didn't have any problem turning Chris on to his connection. Chris had a lot more money than Benny, and he would be able to get a better price on the product. Chris had promised to give

Benny whatever price he was getting the kilos for in return for him brokering the deal.

Once Chris had the product, he began recruiting some of the young boys who had filled the shoes of the brothers who died or went to prison before them. This was the main reason the government would never win the war on drugs. There was always someone to take the place of a fallen soldier.

Chris started taking precautions to protect his home. He had top of the line security systems installed. The young boy with the Cadillac truck, whose name was Gabe became a fixture in his household.

Gabe was about twelve years old when Chris had left. He lived a few doors down from Country and would always be in the street playing. Country took a liking to him and would give him money and buy him food. Chris always did the same.

Gabe emulated Country and Chris. He wanted to be like them. He was the youngest member of Point Blank Mob at fourteen. When Jihad and Crook had been killed and everyone went to prison, Gabe had been left with an opportunity to make an enormous amount of money. Every major hustler was taken off the streets. Gabe was left with an open market and a garage full of drugs, guns, and money that the police hadn't known about. The only reason he knew was because Jihad's partner, Tree used to treat Gabe like his little brother and took him everywhere.

By the time Gabe was eighteen he had bought an Escalade truck, a home, and had enough money to do whatever he pleased. Tree's sister, Love, had hooked him up with her cousin from Detroit who supplied Gabe with a continuous inventory of cocaine. When Chris approached him, Gabe didn't have to think twice. "I'm with you, fam'. Anything you need."

With Gabe on Chris's team, the money began to pour in again. Gabe's soldiers became loyal to Chris, and within months, Chris was running the streets once again. The only thing that bothered Chris was the Russians still hadn't made a move. Why would they allow Chris to build up a resistance? Why not just take him out? He kept replaying Jesus's words. "They want you to build a relationship with your daughter."

It just didn't make sense. Surely by now they would have tried something. Chris had now been out the halfway house for five months. Business was thriving, but he was worried. He didn't know his enemy. Otherwise, he would have started the war himself. He never took the time to investigate Val. He saw no need.

The peace remained for months, and Chris began to relax. Then out of nowhere he got a call that would set it off.

It was late afternoon when his phone rang. He didn't recognize the number, but when he answered, his mother's husband was on the other line sounding hysterical.

"Christopher, you need to get here. Something has happened," his stepfather Gary said.

"What's wrong?" Chris asked. His mother wasn't in the best of health, so Chris was thinking the worst.

"She's gone," Gary said.

Chris pulled his car to the side of the road and sat there stunned. He didn't expect to hear that his mother was gone. Her health wasn't the greatest, but for her to just up and die took Chris by surprise.

"What happened?" Chris asked somberly.

"We don't know. All I know is somebody shot her," Gary said.

Chris couldn't move. Gary's words echoed in his brain, and he felt like his head was going to explode.

"Chris . . . Chris, please just get here." Gary hung up the phone without waiting for a response.

At that moment his phone rang again. Chris answered without looking at the number, "Gary, I'm—"

"Hello, Christopher," the man said on the other end of the phone whose enunciation was without a doubt Russian.

Chris didn't say anything.

"Based on your silence I will assume that you received an alarming phone call. I'm truly sorry about your mother. If it makes you feel any better she died quickly. Just like my granddaughter."

"You motherfucker!"

"Shut up, Christopher. Shut up and listen," Nicholai said as he held the phone out to Misty as she cried out, "Christopher, he's got Autumn."

Chris laid his head against the steering wheel and the tears came. "What the fuck do you want?" he asked.

Nicholai only laughed at Chris's futile gesture. "Do you really think there is anything I want except for you to suffer. Before I kill you, I'm going to take everything you love and crush it. I want you to feel the pain that my family has felt. Then I'll be at peace. Until then . . ."

The phone hung up. Chris pounded the steering wheel of his new 745 BMW. "Please . . . don't do this," he pleaded.

He knew he had to get it together. His first step was to find out what he could about Val's family. He knew Val's maiden name. That was it. He also knew that her father was an attorney with an office in Manhattan. After a few calls, he had an address and he called Gabe. His young soldier answered on the third ring.

"Yo fam', I'm coming to get you," Chris said.

"What's up? You all right?" Gabe asked, noticing the tension in his friend's voice.

"Not at all. I'll rap to you when I get there."

Chris had gotten too relaxed. Now his mother was dead and his wife and daughter were in the hands of a monster. The only thing Chris had to begin was an address to Val's father's law firm on the Avenue of the Americas in New York City. It was time to play offense, but Chris didn't have a lot of time.

When Chris arrived, Gabe was ready. He jumped in the car and immediately hit Chris with a barrage of questions, "My nig, what's up? You cool?"

"These motherfuckers got my daughter, fam'. They got my wife. Dog, they just killed my mother," Chris said.

Gabe looked at his partner. His eyes were puffy and blood shot. He could tell he had been crying. He had no idea how to console a grieving man. He had never dealt with drama on this level and didn't know how to react. He chose his words carefully. "So who exactly got them, fam'? I mean, all you told me is you got some beef, but you ain't ever went into detail."

Chris broke everything down to Gabe as the two men drove to Chris's stash spot and grabbed some traveling money. When Chris finished explaining, Gabe looked at him nervously. "So what you're telling me is we're at war with the Russian mafia."

Gabe couldn't believe what he was saying. He was nineteen years old. He should have been in college, but instead he was in a car traveling to New York to take on an international crime syndicate.

"If you want out I understand," Chris said. "I started this shit, so I have to see it through."

Gabe thought it over for a second. "My nig, I'm here for you. If it's my time then fuck it. I don't got shit out here anyway."

Chris nodded at his man. Then he picked up his phone and dialed his man Tuck in New York. The two men had become close while in the Feds and kept in touch periodically. The call went to voice mail, so Chris left him a message to call back.

Chris wondered how things had gotten so out of control. He remembered as kids him and his man Country playing outside late at night in the courtyard of their Crawford Village housing project. The two boys were always into some form of mischief, but it was never anything serious like prison or death. However, as an adult these two consequences were Chris's everyday nemesis. His actions had brought so much pain to the people that he was supposed to love. Now he found himself driving to New York to save the only thing he had left that meant anything to him. He prayed he wouldn't let them down. He looked over at his man Gabe and asked, "You cool, fam'?"

"Hell yeah," said Gabe as he took a pull on his blunt. The end of the blunt turned a fiery orange as he inhaled the sweet purple chronic into his lungs. He held it for a few seconds and exhaled.

"Remember when I was a kid and how you and Country were always there for me?" Gabe asked.

"Yeah, I remember," Chris replied.

"Man, we didn't have shit. Mom's was so strung out. She used to sell all my shit. She would sell all her food stamps. I loved going to school because at least I got to eat. If it wasn't for you and Country, my ass would have starved."

Chris sat in silence. He had known Gabe's mother was a fiend, but he didn't know that his childhood was that bad. They looked out for Gabe because he was always around and it just felt like the right thing to do. He could never in a million years imagine what his kindness had meant to Gabe.

"Fam', I won't ever forget that. I loved yinz," Gabe said with his Pittsburgh accent. "If it wasn't for yinz, I would have probably starved. So now I'm returning the favor. I'm with you till the casket drops. So regardless what happens I won't have any regrets. It is what it is."

Chris looked at his man and thanked him. He didn't have anyone else to turn to in his time of need. Gabe ran to his side and possibly into what might be his death. Words couldn't begin to explain Chris's gratitude toward his comrade.

As the mile markers passed, Chris pictured his wife Misty and his daughter Autumn. In his mind, they were God's most beautiful creatures. Misty had been there with him through everything. She was a strong woman with loyalty unparalleled. Chris owed her the world and everything in it. He repaid her by letting her down. She had asked him so many times to get out of the game, but he never listened. The game kept calling him and he always answered without considering the consequences. He always said he loved his family, but everyday he chose the streets over them.

He thought about Autumn and how her innocence was being stripped from her at such a young age. If Chris had never pulled the trigger, none of this would be happening. Now that he looked back on the situation, he realized it wasn't worth it nor was it necessary. He could have just walked away. She wouldn't have been able to hurt him. He could have turned his back on the game, but he made a decision based on emotion. And now almost seven years later, it was coming back to haunt him. Misty's cousin, Jesus had always assured him that "Everything you do in the dark will eventually come to light." Chris dismissed the old cliché and didn't take heed to it. Once again it was proven to be true, and now Chris found himself in the middle of a war. Faced with the choice of fight or flight, he made the decision to fight. It felt like a suicide mission, and the deck was stacked against him, but one thing was for sure, Chris was going to take as many of these motherfuckers with him before he died. "Fuck 'em," he said out loud and turned up the radio on the 745i as DMX's "Damien" pumped through the speakers.

"Why is it every move I make turn out to be a bad one/Where's my guardian angel/need one wish I had one/I'm right here shorty and I'm gonna hold you down/And tryin' to fuck all these bitches I'm gonna show you how/"

The song continued to play as Chris zoned out, not overlooking the coincidence of the song. He had made a deal with the devil, and although he had prospered, he was now paying a huge price. Now all deals were off.

The trip to New York took about six hours. They were about to hit the turnpike in Jersey when Tuck finally called back.

"Chris, what's up, good brother?" he asked.

"Nothing good. Yo, I don't really want to rap on this phone, but I'm almost in your neck of the woods. Need some huntin' gear. You think you can hook me up."

Tuck was hesitant at first but finally responded, "What you coming up here to hunt for?"

"Like I said, I really don't want to talk on this phone. Can I just meet you?" Chris asked.

SHAWN 'JIHAD' TRUMP

Tuck knew Chris was a standup guy, so he gave him the address of a little Lebanese hookah spot in Brooklyn called "Kush" that he and his girl always went to. There was a mixed crowd with plenty of people, and they would be able to have some drinks and discuss whatever business they needed to.

Chris arrived at the spot a couple hours later. He had called Tuck and let him know he was there. Tuck arrived about forty-five minutes later. Chris found a seat on the comfortable sofa that had a table situated in front of it. The bar's Moroccan theme and earthly colors intrigued both him and Gabe. Their waitress talked them into a Kush Martini, and although Gabe indulged, Chris declined the hookah. When Tuck finally arrived, Chris stood to greet his friend.

"So what's good?" Tuck asked.

Chris once again explained his dilemma. Tuck sat patiently until Chris finished. "Those are some serious dudes. I've dealt with them here and there, but they make me nervous. I can get you any hardware you need, but fam', you're in some shit. I got a wife and kid that I need to worry about, so after I get you the heat I'm out."

"That's all I want from you. I would never ask you to get in my war. When can I get with you?" Chris asked.

Tuck looked over at Gabe, and then motioned Chris to take a ride with him. "Leave your keys with your man. We'll be back in about an hour."

Chris did as he was told and left with Tuck. They rode to a small apartment building. While they drove, Tuck gave Chris all the information he could. He also offered him some advice, "Bro, I can't begin to imagine what you're going through. But you need to know that you don't got no win. These dudes got armies up here. It's just you and your boy. Why don't you just take your money and run?"

"They got my wife and kid, dog. Without them I'm dead anyway. I need to at least try and save them."

Tuck just shook his head. He knew the position that Chris was in. He also knew deep down inside that nobody was going to live through the ordeal. Chris, his friend, his wife and daughter were all going to die. There was nothing Chris or anyone could do to stop it, but he would still accommodate his friend. At least Chris would die knowing he tried.

Inside the apartment, Tuck retrieved some bags and brought them out to Chris. "Here fam', take what you need."

Chris opened the bag and sorted through the firearms taking out a few pistols for him and Gabe. He also grabbed a Cobray M-11. Tuck put them in a separate bag for him, and Chris asked," How much?"

"Don't worry about it," Tuck replied.

They drove back to the club in silence. Chris called Gabe and asked him to meet him at the car. When they pulled up, Tuck looked at his man. "Good luck, baby boy." Tuck knew he would probably never see Chris again. He wanted to help him in some way, but there was nothing for him to do. He wasn't going to walk into certain death for anybody.

Chris nodded in response and thanked Tuck for the guns. With nothing left to say, he and Gabe jumped in his car and drove to their target.

It was late, so they wouldn't be able to do anything. Chris wanted to do some reconnaissance. He really didn't have a plan except to grab Valerie's father and torture him for information concerning his wife and daughter's whereabouts.

The building wasn't overwhelmingly modern. It was rather simple compared to the neighboring architecture. They had parked the car and set out on foot to scout and plan their attack. There was a sign-in desk, so entry to the office wouldn't be a huge issue. Chris wasn't sure if they knew he was here. He assumed somebody was watching his moves, but how close he didn't know.

After concocting a plan, they returned to their car and drove to the Hilton hotel, which happened to be the first accommodations they saw. The two men retired to their rooms, but neither of them slept easy. The following day weighed heavy on their minds.

When Chris woke up it was dark outside still. The clock on the nightstand read 5:43 a.m. He tried to go back to sleep but couldn't. He grabbed his coat and headed out the door.

He walked through the streets trying to gather his thoughts. People were just starting to hit the streets on their way to work, but Chris didn't notice anybody. He knew he was up against enormous odds, but he didn't have a choice. What kind of man would he be to walk away from his wife and daughter? In prison he had made himself so many promises. He would walk away from the streets and never look back. Instead, he walked out of prison and dug himself deeper than he had ever been.

It was almost 7:30 a.m. when he returned to the hotel and knocked on Gabe's door. His friend answered and let him in. "How'd you sleep?" asked Chris.

"Like shit," Gabe replied. Then he asked, "Yo, fam'. You sure this is what you want to do?"

Chris thought about it before he answered, "No, but what other choice do I have?"

"You can walk away. If they kill us, your daughter and wife will die, too. Maybe you should think about yourself for once. I know it sounds crazy, but all of us don't have to die."

"You're right, bro'. I can't let you do this," Chris said.

"What you mean? You ain't *let* me do nothing. I chose to come," Gabe responded harshly.

"Fam', listen. You got your whole life ahead of you. You got plenty of money. Just do me a favor, walk away. These streets are relentless. I need you to go home. I've thought about this."

"Nigga, I ain't—"

"Stop fam'. Please, just listen to me. I know what I need to do, but I can't let you die over my mistakes," Chris replied.

"So what am I supposed to do? Walk home or something? You got me all the way up to New York then you tell me to leave," Gabe responded.

"I just need them burners out the trunk. Then you can take my car and go. If something happens to me the title is in the glove box."

Gabe wasn't happy with what Chris was doing, but he couldn't argue. Chris just wouldn't listen. As they walked to the car, Chris told Gabe where one of his storage units was. He asked that Gabe take the money to Chris's stepfather to help him with his mother's funeral and anything else he may need. Gary had called Chris's phone a few times wondering where he was. His last message admonished Chris for being cruel and not having enough respect to come when his mother had just been murdered. If Gary only knew that Chris was the one responsible for her death.

When the two men arrived at the car, Chris retrieved the M-11 and tucked it under his coat and stuffed the .45 Smith & Wesson in his waistband. The men embraced and Chris walked away toward the law office.

He covered the distance quickly. When he arrived, the security guard at the desk had him sign in. Chris quickly signed the book and headed for the elevators. The office was on the eighth floor. When the doors opened, Chris walked out and headed to suite 801. When he entered the office it was more than he expected. There were three receptionists, and off to the left were cubicles with more than twenty paralegals all at work. Chris had no idea what to do.

"Sir, can I help you?" the receptionist asked.

Chris hesitated. "I'm here to see Marshall Thomas."

"Your name?" the receptionist asked.

"Christopher Michaels."

"Is he expecting you?"

"I'm sure he is."

"Have a seat." The receptionist lifted her phone and dialed the extension.

After a short wait, Valerie's father emerged. He was in no way intimidating. Nothing compared to what Chris had expected. "Christopher, so good to see you," he said nervously. "Right this way."

Chris followed the man, unsure of what would happen next. He knew why Chris was there. It showed in his demeanor. When they walked in his office, Marshall sat down and Chris took a seat across from him.

"So what pleasure do I owe this visit?" Marshall asked.

"You can stop fucking playing with me like this is a game. Where's my wife and daughter?" Chris asked angrily.

Marshall looked at Chris fiercely, and then spoke in a low, menacing voice. "Who the fuck do you think you're talking to? Don't let my Harvard looks fool you. You are nothing to me. Your hood bravado doesn't mean shit down here, boy. As for your loved ones, you should ask Nicholai. He's the one who has them. He's the one who killed your mother. I wanted no part of it. I know why Valerie died, and I was willing to accept that. If you had not murdered her, somebody else would have."

Chris sat there unable to think of his next move. He responded by lifting his gun and asking, "Where the fuck is my family?"

Marshall looked at Chris and laughed. "Is that the best you can do?"

In a matter of seconds, Chris was around the desk. He grabbed Marshall by the collar of his shirt and smacked him across the mouth with his pistol. Blood sprayed across the desk and Marshall looked up at Chris. "You're a dead man."

Chris was starting to lose control. He was in a law office in the middle of Manhattan. Any continued violence would draw attention, and he would never make it out of the building. If that happened, Misty and Autumn were dead. He released Marshall from his grip and turned his back in defeat and began to walk away. Before reaching the door, he turned to the man and spoke, "I'm sorry for what happened to Val. I'm not proud of the person I was, but I'm not that person any more. I just want my wife and daughter. Please . . . just give me my wife and daughter. I'm the one who killed her, not them."

Marshall looked across his desk. He could taste blood in his mouth. He stared at the man who had killed his daughter, but he couldn't find it in his heart to hate him. He believed that if anyone was responsible for Valerie's death it was Nicholai. He had introduced her to his ways. He despised Nicholai. In the beginning the money was intoxicating. However, Marshall came to understand that Nicholai was a monster and would barter his own daughter for a dollar. He knew that in Nicholai's world the only person who mattered was Nicholai.

"Why would I help you? You took my daughter from me."

"I know what I did. I have to live with it. Your daughter went for her gun. I had no choice," Chris replied.

Marshall let out a sigh. His eyes met the floor and he spoke softly. "They are at Nicholai's warehouse in Port Newark. It's called L&S Shipping Agent Inc. 201A Export Street, Newark," Marshall said.

"Thank you," Chris said as he turned to leave.

"There are probably twenty men there, and all of them are loyal to Nicholai. You don't have a chance."

Chris nodded somberly and said, "I have to at least try."

Marshall watched as Chris walked out of his office toward certain death. Deep down he prayed that Chris would succeed. If Nicholai were dead, Marshall would be able to attain some form of peace in his life.

CHAPTER 30

The first person Chris called when he left Marshall's law office was Gabe. He answered immediately.

"What's good, fam'? Where you at?" Chris asked.

"Standing across the street looking at you, nigga. I know you didn't think I was gonna really leave." Gabe laughed.

Chris looked up and saw Gabe staring at him with a huge smile on his face. He walked across the street and hugged his man. Now that he knew where Misty and Autumn were being held, the plan wasn't so farfetched. He now had hope, and he would need Gabe to pull it off.

"So what happened?" Gabe asked.

"I got an address?" Chris replied.

"Just like that you got an address? You didn't come running out the building, so I know you weren't on any rowdy shit. So what happened?" Gabe asked.

Chris began to explain what had transpired. When he was finished, Gabe looked at him and asked, "Do you think it's the right address? Do you think he would sell Nicholai out that easy?"

"I haven't really thought about it. It was something in his demeanor that makes me want to believe him though."

"Well, I hope you're right. So where we going?"

"Newark."

Chris was glad to have Gabe with him. As the two men drove in silence, the only sound was the navigation system. Chris was deep in thought. He kept praying to Allah. "If you give me my wife and daughter I'll walk away from this mess. Just please give me my wife and daughter."

While Chris prayed, Gabe was trying to psyche himself up. He knew they were up against tremendous odds, but he welcomed the adversity. He had built a name in the streets as a no nonsense person. Chris was just as ruthless. He would place his money on them coming out of the situation victorious, or at least that's what he kept telling himself.

When they arrived to the Port of Newark, both men were in awe. The barges that ran up and down the three rivers in Pittsburgh were nothing compared to the freighters that carried products throughout the world's waterways. There were containers as far as the eye could see.

Chris didn't know what to do next. There was a huge sign that read AP Moller. A man was sitting next to it. Chris pulled his car close and asked for directions. The man was generous and showed Chris the way. Chris drove through the maze of buildings and finally came to his destination. He immediately noticed the guards that patrolled the perimeter of Nicholai's warehouse. They were in uniform and had a standard issued firearm. Not the AK 47 mercenaries that Chris had imagined.

"What you want to do?" Gabe asked as the two men turned into an open space.

"Let's go," Chris replied as he led the way to the warehouse.

On the side of Nicholai's warehouse was a small entrance in the fence, which led to the street. There was no lock. Chris quietly opened the gate and entered the property. Ducking behind containers, Chris made his way to the warehouse. The guards didn't seem to be on high alert which worried Chris. They walked the perimeter casually talking to one another as they passed. *Maybe Misty and Autumn aren't here. Maybe I was wrong in believing Marshall. Maybe Marshall lied,* Chris thought.

He had to go on. Until he knew for sure, Chris could not leave. They found a small entrance in the rear of the building that led to a small break area. There were a few picnic tables and two vending machines. A large man sat at the table eating a sandwich. He never heard Chris approaching.

"Don't fucking move," warned Chris with the gun's barrel pointed directly at the back of the man's head.

The man was too scared to speak.

"I'm going to ask you a simple question. There is a woman and a little girl. I want to know where they are," Chris asked.

"I don't know nothing about no woman and little girl. What are you talking about?" the man asked, trying to figure out what was going on.

"Listen. Your boss, Nicholai. You know him, right?" Chris asked.

"Of course I know him. What does that have to do with me? I just work here."

"He's got my wife and daughter. If I don't get them people are going to die. Do you understand me?"

"Yes. Yes I understand. But I told you that I don't know anything."

Chris believed him. He had to change his line of questioning. "If Nicholai was hiding someone, where would they be?"

The man thought before answering. He knew Nicholai was connected. The man wouldn't hesitate to kill him. Then again, he believed that Chris would kill him, and that threat was immediate. "Upstairs. Nobody is allowed up there but Nicholai and a few other people. Please, just don't kill me."

"Ain't nobody going to hurt you. Just get out of here." Chris removed the firearm from the man's head and headed into the warehouse. The man never looked back. He stood up from the table and walked out to his car, started it up and left. He knew that something bad was about to happen, and he didn't want any part of it.

When Chris walked through the threshold of the warehouse, he noticed everyone at work driving forklifts and pushing hand trucks. Nobody noticed him. He looked around for an entrance to the upstairs that housed offices. There were a few windows, and he could see people as they moved in front of them busy at work. He found the entrance to the stairs that were in the same corridor as the restrooms. He opened the door and walked into his first adversary.

Chris was done talking. He knew Nicholai was in the building and if he couldn't get his family he would die trying. The man was taken by surprise, but Chris was ready. He lifted his weapon and let off a shot. The bullet bore a hole in the man's head as he fell down the steps and came to a rest at Chris's feet.

The gunshots resonated through the passageway and Chris knew they alerted everyone to an intruder's presence. He heard commotion as he took the steps three at a time with Gabe in tow. Chris and Gabe fired at everything moving, and placing the element of surprise in their favor. Gunfire was exchanged, but Chris and Gabe had the upper hand. By the time Nicholai's people formed a resistance, Chris and Gabe evened out the odds. They were still out numbered five to two from what they could tell, but it was a hell of a lot better than eleven to two. They had silenced six men in their initial attack.

THE DEVIL'S GAME

Bullets tore through the walls. Chris and Gabe sought cover in a small office.

"Nicholai, I want my fucking daughter, you pussy!" Chris shouted, trying to coax his enemy into conversation so that he could pinpoint him.

"Christopher," said Nicholai in a long Russian monotone. "You got some big balls coming in here. But why don't you look out here, Christopher. Look at what I got for you."

Chris peered through the door. In the middle of the hallway, Nicholai stood in the center clutching a handful of his daughter's hair. Her mouth was duct taped and her eyes were swollen. Nicholai reached down and yanked the duct tape off her mouth as she hollered out in agony."

"Daddy, please help me. Please help me, Daddy!" Autumn screamed.

Chris fought to breathe. The sight of his daughter's misery was killing him on the inside. He lost it as he came from cover and raised his pistol firing. The first bullet hit Nicholai in his face and knocked him completely off his feet, however, the bullet was not fatal. Nicholai raised the pistol and pointed it in Autumn's direction and Chris fired another round striking Nicholai in the arm causing him to drop his gun.

"Run Autumn!" Chris yelled as he heard gunfire erupt. The hot lead seared his flesh but he continued to battle. He tried to focus. He returned fire and successfully gunned down two more of Nicholai's henchmen. The last man raised his arms in surrender. Nicholai was as good as dead, so his bravado was unnecessary. Gabe took the man's weapon as Chris struggled to keep his balance. He had been shot multiple times and was losing blood. However, he remained conscious as he walked toward Nicholai and stood over his adversary.

"You like playing with people's family," Chris spat.

Nicholai looked up at Chris and smiled. "You know better. My people will come for you. You American piece of trash. Go ahead, motherfucker, kill me. Kill me, motherfucker!"

Honoring Nicholai's last wish, Chris raised the pistol and fired. The hole in Nicholai's head opened up and the life slowly leaked out of him. Chris stood over him unsteady and finally had to balance himself against the wall.

"Gabe, get my daughter," murmured Chris as he tried to lift himself back up.

Gabe helped Chris to his feet and leaned him against the wall as he went to retrieve his friend's family. Chris remained with his gun pointed at Nicholai's last man.

Misty was terrified. Autumn had run back to her and stayed by her side clutching her as the gunfire erupted outside. Then everything went quiet. When Gabe came through the door her eyes went wide. She sat tied to an old wooden chair in a small storage space. Gabe ran to her and began to untie her. He gently removed the tape from her mouth and she fell into his arms.

"Gabe. Thank you. Thank you," she repeated as she turned her attention to Autumn.

At that moment they heard gun fire. Chris put a bullet into the last man's head, choosing to eliminate any additional obstacles instead of showing mercy. He stumbled through the door covered in blood. Gabe and Misty had to run to his side to catch him. They held him up. "We need to get out of here," he said.

"How the fuck we gonna get out of here with all them workers? I know somebody called the police by now," Gabe said.

"Not necessarily. I can still hear them working. All that heavy equipment probably drowned out the shots," said Chris.

THE DEVIL'S GAME

"I know they wear ear plugs because every time I saw somebody come off the floor I saw them take 'em out their ears," Misty added.

"Regardless, we just need to get to the car. I'm losing blood," Chris said.

"Dog, we gotta get you to a hospital," Gabe said.

"Fuck that. Just get me to the car, and I'll call Tuck and see if he can help me. No hospitals. I don't want any police getting involved."

Misty and Gabe looked at one another and jumped into action. Gabe went into one of the offices that appeared to be Nicholai's and grabbed a coat off a rack to cover Chris up. Misty tried her best to clean him up. Autumn stood by her mother's side clutching her leg.

Getting Chris out of the building was a task, but they got by with little attention. It was obvious to anybody that Chris was injured, but it was impossible to see his wounds.

They made it to the vehicle without any resistance, and Gabe flipped open Chris's phone, found Tuck's number and dialed.

"Yo, what's up, kid?" Tuck asked.

"Hey Tuck, it's Chris's boy, Gabe. Yo, Chris is hit up pretty bad. He needs a doctor."

Tuck thought things through. He needed to know the situation before he got involved. "Yo, did he get what he came for? Is shit clear? I can't afford to be getting mixed up in no bullshit."

"We got 'em. And don't worry about them niggaz. We did away with 'em," Gabe replied.

"Where you at, son?" Tuck asked.

"Newark, at the port," Gabe answered.

"Kid, I got you. I got a little broad I fuck with out there who's a vet. I don't know the exact address, but I know it's on Elizabeth Ave. You got a GPS?"

"Yeah."

"All right, punch it in and head that way. Her name is Kristen. I'll tell her you're on your way. She's done stitches on me one night when I was drunk and banged my head. Yo, fam', that's the best I can do. If he's real bad he's gonna have to go to the hospital."

"This nigga will die before he lets me take him to the hospital," Gabe replied.

"Don't ask, just take him," Tuck said.

"I hear you." Gabe hung up the phone and told Misty the address.

Gabe was cautious to obey all the traffic laws. They arrived at the veterinarian's office, and Gabe jumped out of the car. Kristen was waiting and told Gabe to get back in the vehicle and follow her to her home. Gabe did what he was told and five minutes later they were pulling into her driveway.

Chris was barely conscious, and blood now saturated his pants. When they got him inside, Kristen laid a blanket on the floor and they laid Chris down. At first glance Kristen was in shock.

"He's bad. You gotta get him to a hospital," she said, worried that a man was going to die on her living room floor.

"No hospital," Chris said, barely audible.

She tried to gather her thoughts. "All right. Get me some hot water and rags," she said as she opened her bag. "I have to get him cleaned up, so I know what I'm working with."

Gabe did as he was told. Misty sat on the couch clutching her daughter and looking on without emotion. She had been through so much in the last few days. All she wanted to do was go home and get her life back.

Once Kristen cleaned Chris up, she was able to better assess the situation.

"Can you help him?" Gabe asked.

"It looks like he was shot three times and that all the bullets went in and out. I just don't know what happened inside. I can sew him up, but he may be bleeding internally," she said unsure of what to do.

"Just sew me up," Chris mumbled

"But you need blood. You lost a lot of blood," Kristen pleaded.

"I'm still talking to you. So hurry up and sew me up so I don't die," Chris said.

Tears fell from Kristen's eyes. She didn't want to be involved, but Tuck had told her he needed her. He also said Chris was a person that wouldn't forget her and she would be compensated tremendously. She needed the money. She began to sew.

CHAPTER 31

C hris knew he was in a car. He heard the noise of the engine and the cars outside, but he couldn't muster the strength to open his eyes or speak. He remained in this state for the entire trip. When they finally arrived home, he felt Gabe grabbing hold of him and lifting him out of the car. He was carried to the bedroom where he was left to rest.

Over the next few days, Chris was in and out of consciousness. Everything was surreal. A mixture of dreams and nightmares filled his days, but nothing made sense. Misty fed him pain pills, so he didn't feel a thing.

On the third day, Chris awoke for the first time and sat up in his bed. His voice was barely perceptible, but he spoke out, "Misty."

It took him a few tries, but finally he was heard. Misty entered through the door and Autumn was behind her. "Daddy!" Autumn hollered as she ran to her father's side and jumped in the bed.

"Hey baby. How are you?" Chris asked, worried how the events had affected his baby.

"Eww! You stink, Daddy. You need a bath," she said, giggling.

Chris had to agree with her. He smelled horrible. With Misty's help, he got up and made his way to the bathroom. He felt like he had been run over by a truck. Every part of his body was throbbing in pain, but he was grateful to be alive. He wasn't out of the woods yet though. Were the Russians finished with him? Chris wondered what his next move should be.

After showering, he dressed and sat down on the couch next to Misty. He sensed a lot of tension and knew the traumatic events had taken a huge toll on his wife.

"You okay?" Chris asked.

"I will be," Misty said with ice in her voice.

"Listen mama, I know you been through a lot. But this might not be over. I don't know what's gonna happen and if I'm still gonna have to deal with the Russians. We may have to leave."

"Just get some rest. We'll deal with it later. Gabe and a few others are outside. They haven't left since we got back. They are eating us out of house and home, but we are safe for now," Misty said as she got up off the couch and walked away.

Chris watched Misty walk away, feeling hurt that she wasn't taking an interest in him. But he let her go. He looked over at his daughter and asked, "You gonna keep daddy company?"

Autumn nodded and went into the bedroom. Chris dozed off while Autumn lay in his arms watching Dora the Explorer.

Chris had still been asleep when he heard the door to his bedroom open. The room was dark. He reached for Autumn but she was gone. He knew he wasn't alone. He could make out a dark figure. His eyes adjusted to the dark, and he realized it was Misty. "Yo, what you doing?" he asked. She just stood over him and looked down without saying a word.

"Misty, what's wrong with you?"

She lifted the gun and pointed it at him. Chris sat there motionless. His heart skipped a beat, and his eyes shifted from left to right searching for an escape. There was none. "Misty, what the fuck you doing?"

"Why did you do it, Chris? Why!" she screamed.

"Do what? Have you lost your fucking mind? What the fuck are you talking about?" Chris asked, bewildered.

"You know how much he meant to me... and you took his life. You fucking came home after killing my father and held me in your arms! What kind of fucking monster are you? I tried to put it out of my mind. I tried to still love you, but I can't. Every time I look at you now my skin crawls. Just tell me why. Why did you kill him?"

Chris was speechless. He wanted to explain, but nothing came out of his mouth.

"Motherfucker, answer me!" Misty screamed as she pulled the trigger.

The bullet came dangerously close to Chris's head. He heard it whiz by his ear and the down from the pillows fluttered in the air.

"Baby, please," Chris begged as he put his hands in front of his face to shield himself.

"Baby!" Misty hollered as she fired another shot. "Baby? You killed my father, Christopher!" Her body trembled and her eyes watered.

Gabe and the rest of the crew heard the shots and ran in the house. They came running into the bedroom with Autumn behind them. "Mommy, what's going on?" she asked visibly shaken.

THE DEVIL'S GAME

At that moment Misty realized that it wasn't worth it. She threw the gun on the bed, grabbed Autumn, and walked out. Chris heard the door close and just sat up in the bed and swung his feet over the side.

"What the fuck was that about? You want me to go grab her?" Gabe asked.

"Nah, let her go." Chris was stunned that she had somehow found out about Rico.

"You okay, fam'?"

"Just give me a minute, fam'. I gotta figure this shit out," Chris responded.

CHAPTER 32

O ver the next few weeks Chris healed up quickly. He was still in a lot of pain, but his heart hurt more than anything. He had spoken to Misty once, and she informed him that Nicholai had asked her how she could love a man so much who had killed her father. He told her everything. Nicholai did it to torture her. He knew the pain it would cause.

Chris had talked to Tuck and thanked him for his help. He invited him and Kristen down, and when they got there Chris compensated each of them with fifty-thousand dollars.

Chris continued to do business but he was gradually separating himself from the streets. Gabe was going to be the man. That was his dream, and Chris understood it. At one time Chris had those same street dreams, but he learned the hard way that they only ended as nightmares. He had more money than he could spend. However, he had lost everyone that he loved. He prayed that Misty would forgive him and come home, but he didn't count on it.

He spent most of his time opening his detail shop back up. He knew if Misty was going to come home he would have to leave the game alone completely. He found a nice place in the Overbrook section of Pittsburgh and signed the lease. The last week had been spent getting supplies and ordering signs. He planned to open up the following month on the first, and at that time the game would be completely behind him.

The time to open had come. Chris threw a big cookout with free food and refreshments. Everyone came out to celebrate the event. He prayed Misty would show up but she never did. His calls went unanswered. She wouldn't even let him see Autumn. He didn't blame her.

Officer Green became an intricate part of Chris's life helping him stay in line. He knew that Chris had not just walked away from the game like that. He understood that change takes time, and he gave Chris his space. He heard through the streets about Chris's episode in New Jersey. Criminals always believed that they got away with so much, but the truth was the police usually knew what was going on... The problem was proving it. Officer Green drove out to Chris's home to visit him and they had a long talk. Chris seemed to be receptive, and it proved true when out of nowhere Chris called him and asked for his help. It gave Officer Green a sense of fulfillment to help his son's best friend get through his troubles. Chris was lost without his family. He had lost everything, and putting the pieces back together was hard. He needed a father, and with nobody else to turn to he sought out the officer. In return, Officer Green offered his secrecy and never violated that oath. He helped Chris work through all of his issues to establish a clean slate.

Chris wished he could change so many things. So many times the streets had him doing things to hurt the people he loved. In his mind, he was doing those things for his family, but in reality he was hurting them. He had destroyed so many lives. He had destroyed families and dreams. However, he couldn't take it back. Chris couldn't dwell on the past and drown in his regrets. He would have to move on.

Over the next six months the detail shop thrived, grossing almost three thousand dollars a week with little overhead. Chris was negotiating a deal with a real estate agent that would allow him to open up two additional locations. Everything was going great.

He locked up the garage for the night and headed towards his vehicle. As he approached his car he saw Beverly's Mercedes round the corner. It came to a stop in the parking lot next to him and Misty got out of the vehicle. Chris stood there staring at his wife. He wanted to run to her, but he controlled his emotions.

"What's up, mama? How are you?" he asked.

"As good as I can be. How you been?" she asked.

"Just working. The shop is doing great."

"I see that. I've been watching you on Facebook." She laughed.

The sound of her laughter was comforting. "So you're stalking me?" he asked playfully.

"I don't do no stalking, papi. Just checking to see how you are. You are my husband, right?"

"Last time I checked," Chris replied.

"That's good, papi, 'cause we're going to need you. Your kids need their father."

"And I need--- wait---- what do you mean *kids*?" Chris asked, looking dumbfounded.

Misty stepped away from the car and walked around the front to meet Chris. Chris watched as his wife made her way toward him. He now could see her stomach was a mound of expectancy. "What... when..?"

Chris struggled to get the words out, but he was in shock.

"I found out shortly after I left. I'm eight months, papi. I'm due next month," she said.

Chris ran to his wife and grabbed her. He didn't want to let go. Tears ran down his face as he apologized to her over and over. "I'm sorry, mama----. I'm so sorry."

"Papi. Papi, look at me," Misty said as she grabbed Chris's face.

He looked down at his wife and gave her his full attention.

"Christopher, I don't want to know what happened. I know whatever you did you did for a reason. I love you with all my heart, and even though you are responsible for causing me more pain than I could have ever imagined, I love you more than I have ever loved anyone. You have given me a precious daughter, and now I pray for a healthy son."

"We're having a son?" Chris asked.

She smiled and kissed her husband. The couple stood in the parking lot of his shop and embraced.

Misty pulled away. "Chris, please don't ever hurt me again. If I ever think you have returned to the streets I promise I will walk away and never look back. Do you understand me? I can't live like that anymore. Our children deserve better, I deserve better, and most importantly you deserve better."

Chris shook his head in understanding and looked into Misty's eyes. "I promise, mama."

"Then let's go get our daughter," she said.

Chris jumped in his car and followed Misty to her mother's house. When they arrived, Autumn came running out of the house and met Chris at his car. He couldn't believe he had chosen the streets over his daughter so many times. How he could have ever taken the chance of losing her was beyond him.

Misty's mother came out and hugged Chris, obviously not knowing that he was responsible for Rico's death. "Christopher, whatever happened is none of my business. I just hope you guys work it out. I missed you, baby."

"I missed all of you," he said.

"Well, you better appreciate what you have," Ms. Beverly said. Her daughter walked out of her house, hugged her, and threw her bags in the car. Chris carried Autumn to the car and buckled her in.

During the ride home little was said as Chris reflected on everything that had transpired. He now had everything he wanted. He was able to free himself from the repetitive cycle of the streets. There would be no more prison or death. For Chris it was over. He was finally a free man, and as far as he was concerned, the game could call on somebody else.

CHAPTER 33

A month had passed and every day that Chris woke up next to Misty was a cherished one. He showered them with love and prayed he would never be without them again.

Before going to work, Chris cooked his two favorite ladies and his son breakfast. As they sat at the table eating, he realized that all the money in the world could never compare to these moments in terms of happiness. Having to go to work, Chris stood up and excused himself. He planted a kiss on his children's foreheads and hugged Misty good-bye.

"Daddy loves yinz," he said to the kids before leaving.

As he drove to work, Chris thought about everything he had been thru. The sacrifices he made. He thought about Country often and visited his grave regularly. The game had taken so much from him, but in reality he still missed it. It was hard not to think about it, especially with Gabe and the other hustlers frequenting his shop. He missed the rush more than he missed the money, mostly because he was still doing well financially. The money he accrued in the game would last him for a very long time.

Turning into his shop, Chris was immediately pulled from his thoughts. Parked in front of the first bay was a black

Denali with dark tinted windows, which Chris suspected was some form of law enforcement, most likely the Feds.

Chris turned his BMW into the parking space beside his garage and got out. As he did, a man got out of the passenger's side of the truck and proceeded to intercept Chris before he entered the building.

The white man with a thin build stood six-two and weighed not more than 180 pounds. His short brown hair was cut neatly, and he was dressed in a Louis Vuitton button down, brown slacks and brown Ferragamo shoes.

Not sensing a threat, Chris extended his hand. "Can I help you?"

The man took Chris's hand and shook it firmly, "I hope so, Christopher. I've been looking for you for some time now," he replied.

The sound of the man's voice sent a shock through Chris's body. He stared at the man, obviously stunned. He thought they had forgotten about him. Months had passed without a response to Nikolai's death. But the man's Russian accent assured Chris that he was naïve believing that there would be no repercussions. The Russians were here and they caught Chris slipping.

"Would you like to go inside?" Chris asked.

The Russian man nodded as he followed Chris inside. Chris walked to his office and had a seat at his desk. He offered the Russian a seat. The man glanced at his surroundings, and then stared at Chris and smiled.

"All this time I have been wondering which one of our enemies was responsible for my associate's death. In the end I find out it's nothing more than a small city hustler."

Chris just stared at the man.

"My organization was completely unaware of the issues between Nikolai and yourself. It was just recently brought to our attention." He paused, thinking about his words before he spoke.

"Christopher, Nikolai was a very reckless man and a source of tremendous irritation to my boss. However, he was also a man who made a lot of money for us, and now with him gone it has created a loss of income that we are not happy about. This is the only reason you are alive right now. In a sense, you did us a favor."

"So why are you here?" Chris asked.

"Money, of course. You are responsible, and now Nikolai's debts are your debts. In all fairness, we are willing to forgive our past losses... start fresh, if you will."

Chris responded nervously, "I'm not in the game no more. Nikolai kidnapped my wife and daughter..." The Russian cut him off before he finished.

"And you killed his granddaughter. That seems to be a fair trade."

"She was a fucking rat!" Chris yelled.

"Even so, these issues are irrelevant. It's already been decided," said the Russian.

"What has?"

"That you now work for us. You will continue where Nikolai left off."

"What if I say no?" Chris asked.

"Then you and your family die. That simple," said the Russian as he rose to leave. He walked out the door and said over his shoulder, "I know you've been a good boy. We are reasonable people, so we don't expect a miracle overnight. Nikolai's drug operation brought us $2 million per month.

You have six-months to do the same. In my truck there are fifty kilograms of cocaine. I will be back in exactly one month for our money. At that time you will have a hundred more."

Chris's heart raced as he followed the Russian outside. The driver got out of the truck and tossed Chris the keys and waved to another vehicle that Chris hadn't noticed. The Russian turned to Chris. "Eight-hundred thousand, Christopher. Please don't let it be a penny less. And you can keep the truck... call it an incentive."

The other car pulled up, and the two men got in without another word. Chris stared at them hopelessly as the car pulled away.

CHAPTER 34

The phone on Gabe's nightstand continued to ring. He knew it was Chris's ringtone but thought he just wanted some help at the shop and having just come home at 4 a.m., it wasn't happening. It wasn't till the fourth consecutive try that Gabe reached for the phone knowing that Chris wouldn't keep blowing him up if it wasn't important.

"Hello," Gabe answered groggily

"I'm at your door," Chris said.

Gabe noticed the tension in Chris's voice and hurried out of bed and moved towards the door. As soon as Gabe opened the door, Chris pushed past him trembling.

"Dog, I got drama. I fucked up good. These pussies got me by the balls."

"What? Slow down. Who?" Gabe asked.

"Fucking Russians," Chris replied.

Hearing those words sent Gabe to the window to look out at his parking lot. He retrieved his gun as he asked "Where they at? Did they follow you?"

"It's not that type of drama," Chris said.

"What other kind is there?"

"The kind that goes down when you inherit the devil's debt," Chris said solemnly. Gabe sat and listened as Chris filled him in. What was Chris's curse was Gabe's blessing.

"Nigga, is you trippin'? They just gave you fifty birds. We're set," Gabe said, becoming excited at the thought of a major connect.

"I don't want this shit. I left this shit alone. I just got my family back," Chris replied. "I just had a son."

"Let me rock that shit. I'll take all that shit."

Chris looked at Gabe and chose his words carefully, hoping not to offend his friend. "Fam', this is a whole other level. You're doing five to ten kilos a month. Fifty kilos just don't sell themselves. And we only got a month. On top of that I will have to do a hundred next month. If we don't get their paper when they want it, we die and probably our families will die also."

"What other choice do we have?" Gabe asked, already knowing the answer.

Chris realized there was only one option. Now the major question was whether or not he should tell Misty. Their son David, named after Country, was only seven-months old. If Misty left him, who would teach his son to be a man? But if he didn't do what the Russians told him to do… he wouldn't have a son.

"Meet 'em at the shop in two hours, fam'. I have to go see my wife," Chris said as he walked out of Gabe's house.

As Chris drove home, he tried to find the words to piece together an argument that would make Misty understand his dilemma. Regardless, he wouldn't lie to his wife. It was almost half an hour before Chris got to the house. When he arrived, he found Misty lying with his son on the couch, both asleep. Autumn sat in the chair watching Dora the Explorer, as if it was the only thing that mattered in the world.

He took a seat on the edge of the couch and rubbed his son's back and studied his wife. Her features were perfect. He couldn't stand the thought of losing her. Chris prayed she would understand.

"Baby," he said as he nudged Misty. She opened her eyes and smiled.

"What are you doing home?" she asked as she stretched, trying to loosen up from her sleep.

"We need to talk," Chris replied as he looked at Autumn and said, "Hey baby, can you come watch your brother for daddy, so me and mommy can talk?"

Autumn watched the baby as Chris took Misty's hand and led her outside. It was fall. The leaves were starting to change. A warm breeze filled the air with smells of nature that surrounded their home. The sound of the stream that ran behind the home was soothing. It would be the perfect setting for a romantic lunch at the picnic table, but instead Chris sat Misty down with a nervous look on his face. Misty knew something bad had happened.

"Baby, what's wrong?" she asked.

Chris took a deep breath and began to explain. As he spoke, he searched his wife's face for any indication of the feelings but she remained stoic.

"So what are you going to do?" she asked once he finished speaking.

"The only thing I can," Chris replied.

"And that is?"

"Get these boys their money." Chris waited for her to scream. Waited for her temper to flare, for her to get up and leave, taking the kids. Her silence made his stomach turn.

"Whatever it takes to protect our family, do it, papi. I ain't going nowhere."

CHAPTER 35

W e about to get this money," Gabe said excitedly staring at the fifty kilos sitting on the floor in an air conditioner box. Chris just tried to ignore him as he searched his phone and compiled a list of all the dudes he planned to holler at over the next few days. The good thing about having done federal time was that he met a lot of guys who were getting serious money. A lot of them had been released and remained in touch. His first call was to his man Milk in Columbus. They had been cellmates for about a year during his bid. When Chris called and told him indirectly that he had them things for twenty thousand, Milk couldn't get on the highway fast enough. The same went for Yah Yah in Atlanta, Face in Lexington, Tu in Morgantown, Salim in Delaware, and last but not least, his man Tuck from New York. He also got at his man, Charlie Bell from Pittsburgh who after doing time together, Chris trusted with his life. Chris didn't intend on dealing with too many people from Pittsburgh. He would let Gabe run through whatever was left. The least exposure Chris had to the streets, the better. He still had a business to run. He had become a pillar to both his community at home and the city of Pittsburgh where his business was located. Most importantly, Chris had his family and didn't ever want his children to view him as a criminal.

The weeks passed by. With Chris's out of state connections buying up all the product, only a week went by before they had the Russians' money. There was enough *blow* left over to last Gabe for the month. This allowed Chris to focus on his deal with the realtor.

He was opening two new car detail locations. One in Penn Hills, and one by his home in Monongahela. He had closed on the properties and was in the process of having them renovated to suit his needs.

Misty had taken a break from teaching to raise the kids. She would be running the establishment in Monongahela, allowing her to spend time with the kids and work at the same time. Chris had a playroom added along with a comfortable office. This would serve as the company's headquarters. Misty was more than qualified to handle the task, and Chris silently prayed that Misty would get comfortable enough to forget about returning to teaching.

Chris's mother had worked two jobs to support him. He knew she loved him, but she was never there to show it. Therefore, he sought his love and parental guidance in the streets. He wanted better for his kids. Chris had been working twelve to fifteen hour days since the shop opened. He could have easily paid someone, but he wanted not just his money, but his sweat supporting his success.

The time finally came to exchange money for drugs with the Russian whom Chris learned was named Alex. The Russian was impressed that Chris handled the fifty kilos without any problems. They watched for almost two months after Marshall mentioned Chris's existence in one of their meetings, believing that they were already aware of the issue that stemmed from Valerie. However, he found that Nikolai was keeping more than just information from the mob's hierarchy. Apparently, Nikolai was also branching off into other unspoken illicit activities without giving the organization their due. This was the reason Chris was still breathing, but he didn't know that. After watching him, they realized that Chris was no longer involved in the drug game. They were skeptical about doing any business with him, but after doing an extensive background check they realized that Chris would be an asset.

The transaction went smoothly, and Chris was becoming less concerned about being pulled back into the game. He sold twenty kilos to Gabe at his price and the other thirty were sold at twenty thousand a pop for a profit of one hundred twenty-thousand. The hundred kilos he just gained control of would just double those numbers.

By the time the third month came, Chris was requesting one-hundred and fifty kilos. The out of state connects were proving a very profitable network, and during an evening with his crew, Chris proposed a toast, actually thanking the Feds for locking him up. Misty having been present, stared angrily at Chris and the following morning she didn't bite her tongue.

"Did you have fun last night?" Misty asked.

Chris looked at his wife over a bowl of cereal and gave her a simple shrug

"It was just another night."

"Are you out of your fucking mind?" she asked angrily.

Chris was taken aback by her aggressive demeanor.

"What's wrong with you?"

"Papi, you can't be serious. What's wrong with me? Proposing a toast to the Feds for locking you up. You don't sound like a man who is being forced to sell drugs to protect his family. You sound like a fucking drug dealer. You make me sick. I trusted you."

"Baby, I don't want this. I don't need to do this, but if I have to do it you best believe I'm going to make the best of it," Chris replied.

"Why can't we just leave? Turn everything over to Gabe. He loves this shit, papi."

"And go where? It's the Russian mob, mama. They are everywhere. I made the deal with the devil, so it's me that has to pay his debt."

Misty understood her husband's predicament, but she couldn't continue to live like this. She was thinking about her kids. If Chris went back to prison or got himself killed, it would destroy them. Autumn was attached to him at the hip. Misty knew what she would have to do, but if it didn't work out then Chris would never forgive her.

CHAPTER 36

A few weeks had passed since Misty blew up at Chris. Misty had been keeping to herself a lot, and Chris was feeling the pain of her distance. Now Chris was on the phone listening to his man Nitty, wondering if he should have paid more attention to his wife's concerns. Two days prior, Chris's man Charlie, known also as CB, had been subjected to a raid, and Chris was just now finding out... from someone else.

"Did they find anything?" Chris asked.

"I doubt if they found anything, but CB don't let his strap leave his hip. I know they had to find a gun at least," Nitty answered.

Nitty hated going behind Charlie's back and telling Chris. They had grown up together, but Nitty didn't believe Charlie's story. The police didn't just run in your house, catch you with a gun, and let you go. Charlie was a felon. He admitted to Nitty that they found the gun, but told a bullshit story that the gun was registered to his girl. Nitty knew that shit didn't matter. Nitty didn't tell Chris the whole story, but just enough to wake him up, so that he would be careful. If it turned out Charlie was snitchin', Nitty would be in Chris's good graces. If Charlie's story came up true, he may be able to salvage their friendship.

Before getting off the phone, Chris thanked Nitty and promised to keep their conversation a secret. He picked the phone back up and called Gabe.

"What's good?" Gabe answered.

"Come to the shop," Chris replied, and then hung up

Gabe knew something was wrong. He was ten minutes away from the detail shop in Overbrook at a bar called Jose and Tony's. He had just left there an hour ago. *What the fuck happened?* Gabe took one last bite of his burrito and threw everything into the trash. It was the middle of December and snow was falling. The roads were developing a thin layer, but that wouldn't deter Gabe from doing double the speed limit. He pushed the brand new 2005 Mercedes S430 automatic through traffic, impressed with the handling that the all-wheel drive provided.

"Who said money don't buy happiness?" Gabe laughed to himself as he turned up the stereo letting that Young Jeezy beat through his speakers. "When you're from where I'm from you gotta get it how you live."

Chris was waiting outside the shop when Gabe pulled up. He jumped in the car with Gabe.

"Let's go to the shop in Monongahela. It will give us time to talk."

Gabe responded by putting the car in drive and heading south on Route 51.

"So what's up?" Gabe asked.

"We might have a rat," Chris answered.

"Huh?" Gabe jerked his head up, watching Chris instead of the road.

"CB," Chris said and then added, "watch the road." Gabe almost swerved into the car next to him.

THE DEVIL'S GAME

Chris brought Gabe up to date on the situation with Charlie. He knew something wasn't right. If the police raid your house you let the connect know. And if you didn't there were two possible reasons. Number one: You were scared the connect would cut you off. Number two: You were trying to set the connect up. Either way Charlie tried to cop without telling Chris about the raid. Charlie's involvement was done. Eight years ago Chris would have killed him, but things were different now.

With everything that was happening Chris knew it was time to speak with the Russians about letting Gabe take over. They wouldn't be losing anything, and Gabe was more than capable of handling the affairs. He wanted to let Misty know that he was going to try and work things out. He prayed Alex had come to trust Chris's judgment, but he couldn't be certain. He looked at Gabe. "I want out, fam," Chris said.

"Out of what?"

"Out of this game. My heart's not in it. I'm not gonna trade my family for the game."

"What about the Russians?" Gabe asked.

"What about them?"

"They won't let you just walk away," Gabe stated

"They may, if someone takes my place," Chris said. "Are you ready?"

Gabe thought to himself for a second, "Yeah I'm ready for whatever."

They drove in silence the rest of the way. Chris was thinking about what he would say to Alex. Gabe was thinking about all the money he stood to make. Pulling into the shop, he saw Autumn playing with David. It brought a huge smile to his face. David was now fifteen months old and walking.

Autumn lugged him around everywhere. Even though there was only an inch of snow on the ground, Autumn was showing her little brother how to make snow angels.

"Daddy!" Autumn yelled. She ran from the fenced in area beside the shop that Chris had set up for the kids to play outside. Chris lifted his princess, who was getting bigger every day. He gave her a kiss and set her down, so he could give David some attention. David kept hitting Chris in the leg and looking up at his father, like: "Can I get some love too?"

At that moment, Chris knew he didn't have an option. He had to leave the game. It was time for him and Alexander to talk.

CHAPTER 37

In his mind, the meeting with Alexander went smoothly. He raised numerous points that showed his participation wasn't necessary, so when Alex spoke Chris was thrown off his square some and when Alex continued to speak the dialogue became tense.

"No," Alex said.

"Huh?" Chris replied. "Why not?"

"Because, I said so."

"Gabe is more than capable of running things. I'll give him all my people," Chris said, pleading his case.

Alex was tired of explaining himself. Since Chris couldn't understand no, Alex spoke bluntly. "I'm not doing business with a nigger."

"What the fuck did he just say?" Chris thought, seething inside, but he didn't allow his temper to show. It would have been a sign of weakness.

"Alex, I'm going to ask that you respect me as I do you. My wife is half-black, which makes my children fall under that same umbrella."

"Christopher, I didn't refer to your wife and children. You chose to include them. However, I'll entertain you with a lengthy response to your request. You want me to drop one-hundred fifty kilos off to your partner Gabe, who as we speak is probably standing on a corner somewhere next to his hundred thousand dollar car, with his twenty thousand dollar chain in a hoodie and work boots smoking weed and shooting dice telling everyone who will listen that he's a drug dealer. Now there's you: successful businessman, loyal husband and father, charitable, who is only selling drugs to protect his family. Gabe is a liability because of his ignorance and utter stupidity. You are an asset that I'm not willing to trade."

"So when is it over?" Chris asked as his stomach tied in knots.

"The devil's debt is paid when you finally go and meet him. You chose the game Christopher, it didn't choose you, so live with it." Alex got up and collected the 2.4 million dollars that Chris had in two duffle bags. He walked out leaving another one hundred and fifty kilos behind.

"Fuck!" Chris yelled. He slammed his fist on the desk and then ran his hands over his head looking down in frustration. Chris was stuck. He tried praying. He tried negotiating, but it didn't work. He was in with the Russians and they weren't willing to let go. Now he had to tell his man that he wouldn't be taking Chris's place. Gabe would be upset, but Chris would offer him fifty percent of the shipments and supply him with the customers to move the work in time. He considered giving Gabe everything, but what Alex had said struck a chord. Gabe was too open with his business. Eventually, it would be his downfall, and Chris didn't want to go down with him. Chris had always kept his distance because of this. He loved Gabe like a brother, but they were rarely seen together in public. Chris couldn't turn everything over to Gabe. If something were to go wrong, it would endanger Chris's family.

At the thought of his family, Chris started to really stress. He promised Misty things would be all right and that he planned to get out. She wasn't quite as optimistic as him, but the news was still going to crush her. As Chris began to pick up the phone and call Gabe, the phone rang.

"Immaculate Detail," Chris answered.

"What's up, baby? I need to get my ride touched up like usual."

"Charlie fucking Bell," Chris thought. He was waiting for a call ever since Nitty told him about the raid.

"What's up, CB? Anything new?" Chris asked, giving Charlie an opportunity to tell him about the raid.

"I've been out of town," Charlie said. "When do you have something available?"

"Saturday at one," Chris said and hung up the phone. A sense of paranoia surrounded Chris. There was enough cocaine in his garage to put him away for life. He went out into the garage bay area and threw the three large boxes into the truck and left. He dialed Gabe as soon as he pulled out. There wasn't any answer. Chris tried a few more times before Gabe answered.

"What's good?" Gabe asked.

"Where you at?"

"Out the Port fucking with Punchy," Gabe replied.

Punchy was one of Gabe's people, but he had been around since Chris and Gabe hooked up and started getting money. Chris trusted him.

"Yo, bring him with you and meet me at your spot. I'm gonna be there in ten minutes."

Chris hung up and headed to Gabe's, a small ranch styled home in Pleasant Hills. It was the best place to sit down and talk. And it was located only fifteen minutes from Chris's home in McKeesport and the shop on Overbrook. Its long driveway would allow them to see a car coming from a distance. There was also 2.5 acres of land, plenty of places to hide the drugs until Chris got rid of them. Chris didn't know for sure if Charlie was telling, but he wasn't taking any chances.

Chris pulled in and Punchy and Gabe were only minutes behind him.

"You all right?" Gabe asked. The look on Chris's face told him something bad had happened. Punchy sat beside them remaining silent.

"Fucking CB called me as soon as the Russians dropped the work off. I don't know if it was a coincidence or what."

Gabe didn't know what to say. He blurted out, "Were you followed?"

"Am I an asshole? Would I be sitting in your driveway with a hundred fifty keys if I thought I was followed?"

Punchy's jaw dropped. He knew Chris and Gabe were getting serious money, but damn. He just sat there and kept his mouth shut.

"Nah, my bad," Gabe replied, sorry for having offended his man.

"Yo, this shit is crazy," Chris said as the three of them walked into the house and sat down. Chris let them get comfortable. "It's Tuesday. We got to clean house before Saturday. If we have to, we'll deliver this shit ourselves."

"Why don't we just kill his punk ass," Gabe stated rather than questioned.

"If we kill him it really gets hot. And the Russians won't give a shit. They are gonna still want their money."

"Russians?" Punchy asked.

Gabe just looked at him and shook his head. "Long story," Gabe said.

"Look, call your people and I'll call mine. Let them know we are going out of town. Bring what they got, and we'll front the rest. We'll just send someone for the rest of the paper in a week or two," Chris said, making up a plan as he went along.

"That's a lot of shit you're gonna be frontin'," Gabe said.

"Fuck it. If I can get half I'd be happy. Everyone ain't going to fuck up. Hopefully, nobody will. I'd rather lose money than my freedom. Get that shit out of our hands, and we don't have to worry about them finding shit."

The plan was set, so Gabe and Chris got busy. Gabe was running the shit out of Punchy. The next couple of days were almost without sleep. Chris would get in late, spend some time with the kids and Misty and be gone early the next morning. Misty had finally had enough. By the time Thursday arrived, she flipped out.

"What the fuck is going on, papi? You barely got time for us and when you do your mind is somewhere else. You're acting like you got another bitch."

I had a 150 bitches, Chris thought and almost smiled knowing there were only ten left. Chris had Gabe front them out to the dudes he fucked with. Chris had $1.7 million of the Russians' money that he spread out over a few storage units. He could deal with the possibility of the police finding his money if something happened, but they wouldn't find any drugs if they came.

"Mama, you know I don't got another bitch, so watch your mouth. I just got a lot going on," Chris replied, not wanting Misty to worry.

"What you got going on that you don't trust me?" she asked, feeling hurt by his comment.

Chris always told her almost everything. The fact that Chris wasn't sharing his problem with her was tearing her apart, so Chris told her his plan. Tears filled her eyes. She tried to hold them back for his sake, but they began to fall.

"Papi, are we ever going to be free?"

"I don't know," Chris replied. He held his wife close.

CHAPTER 38

O n Saturday morning, Chris was detailing the Denali that Alex had given him. His BMW was horrible in the snow, but the Denali drove through anything. It was a nice addition to his garage. For once, Gabe, who usually slept late, was up helping.

"So dog, you never told me what happened with Alex. We been so focused on CB, I forgot to ask."

Chris didn't know how to respond honestly without having Gabe trying to blow Alex's brains out, so he kept it simple. "My debt, my problem, my job."

"What the fuck does that mean?" Gabe asked.

"They ain't with it. But I got you, fam'. Next trip, I'm going to give you half the load at my price. I'll let you deal with Milk and Yah. We'll just split this shit fifty-fifty."

Gabe shrugged it off like it was cool, but inside he was saying "Fuck Alex!" But what Chris did was some real shit, so fuck it, he would keep his mouth shut and keep getting money. Everybody thought he was the man anyway. Very few people knew Chris still hustled. He kept that shit well hidden. Gabe loved how the hood glorified him. *Dudes kiss my ass and the bitches kiss my dick*, he thought and started laughing.

SHAWN 'JIHAD' TRUMP

At around 12:30, Charlie knocked on the garage door. Chris and Gabe had finished the Denali and were watching a Kevin Hart stand up laughing their asses off.

"Pussy's early," Gabe said.

Without a response Chris rose from his seat and hit the switch to open the garage. Charlie stood there with a smile.

"What's good, baby boy?" he said as he bumped fists with both Chris and Gabe.

Chris backed away to let him in and hit the switch to close the door. The sound of the door closing behind him made Charlie uneasy, and Chris could sense it. He and Gabe stared at CB waiting for him to speak. He looked uneasy as he shifted his feet before he finally spoke.

"You got ten of them for me?" Charlie asked.

Chris didn't respond. Gabe walked over to a table against the wall and lifted a contraption off it. He made his way over to Charlie, who eyed him suspiciously.

"Ten what?" Gabe asked.

"What you think? Ten kilos," Charlie replied.

"You ever see that shit on HBO? *The Wire? That's my shit!* "*Gabe said,* not giving Charlie enough time to respond. "Especially when that little bitch, Snoop be offing people with that nail gun. You know, all them fucking rats and shit."

Charlie knew he was in trouble. Chris and Gabe knew about the set up. They probably thought he was setting them up right now, but he wasn't. He had set some out of town chump up who didn't have any business hustling in Pittsburgh. Somehow it got back to them though.

"Yo, what's up, Gabe?" Charlie asked nervously.

Gabe walked up on him. Charlie began to sweat as Gabe whispered in his ear and placed the nail gun to his chest at the same time. "Strip, pussy."

"Don't do this, fam'. You think I'm dumb enough to be on some wild shit? I would never cross yinz," Charlie begged.

Gabe wasn't listening, so Charlie began to strip. He had a gun in his waistband. Gabe removed it. Charlie stood in front of the two men, shaking. Chris took the clothes and walked them into the office. They were confident that Charlie wasn't wired. The fact that he was armed led Chris to believe it wasn't a set up. No Feds had come busting in to rescue him either.

"You got something to tell me?" Chris asked.

"What you mean?"

"What do I mean?" Chris asked as he took Charlie's gun from Gabe and placed it on his temple. "How about them boys kicked your door in but let you go. Start there, motherfucker."

"Ch-Ch-Chris. It's not like that," Charlie pleaded.

"Fam', you got one more chance to explain, or I'm cancelling your subscription," Chris said sternly.

He hadn't intended to kill Charlie. There weren't any guns at the shop in case it was a set up. The nail gun was only a prop to intimidate Charlie. Now with Charlie's gun in his hand, Chris tasted blood.

"I got some nigga, Pooh, from Detroit. I would never set you up. I told them I was grabbing off him and then set him up. Who gives a fuck about them pussies from out of town?" Charlie argued.

Chris just shook his head in disgust as Gabe stepped up and fired the nail gun twice into Charlie's head.

"What the fuck you do that for?" Chris asked.

"Nigga, Pooh owed me twenty grand. Now I know why he didn't answer my calls." Then he kicked Charlie and cursed. "Fuckin' punk!"

Chris walked away shaking his head. "Get his bitch ass out of here. I ain't digging shit either. It's fucking thirty degrees outside."

"Fuck digging. I'm about to barbeque his ass and feed him to the dogs."

Chris couldn't believe this shit. Dude's kept thinking that if a person told on somebody it didn't matter as long as it wasn't them. To Chris, a rat was a rat and he wasn't fucking with them.

CHAPTER 39

A few hours had passed. Gabe wrapped Charlie up in a tarp with a gun and his belongings and then loaded him into the truck. Gabe's home was secluded enough, so he wouldn't have any problems making the body disappear. Chris was scrubbing the floor when Mister came in the side door.

"What's going on, Chris?" Mister asked.

Something about Country's dad wasn't right. His posture and words seemed aggressive. Chris had never lost sight that Country's dad was a cop, one, who for years was an enemy. So even though they were friends, Chris was always careful.

"How you doing, Chris?" he asked.

"I'm cool," Chris responded.

"You got something you need to talk about," Mister asked.

"Nah. I'm good. What's up?"

It happened so fast Chris was caught off guard. Mister grabbed Chris by the shirt and pinned him against the wall.

"Boy, after everything I've done for you. You don't trust me. You're gonna go behind my back and renege on your promise. I trusted you, son. You make me sick," Mister hollered as he released Chris and turned his back.

"Yo, what the fuck is wrong with you?" Chris asked.

"What's wrong with me? Maybe the fact that a kid I've been supposedly helping, is still running around selling drugs. How's that for starters?"

Chris was stunned. He wasn't fucking with anyone in the Port, so he wasn't sure how Mister knew but it worried him.

"It's not what you think," Chris replied.

"It's exactly what I think. I know all about it. The Russians," Mister emphasized.

How the fuck does he know about the Russians? Only he and Gabe really knew shit. Chris just stood there speechless. Mister realized he wasn't going to get an answer, so he dropped the bomb.

"Misty told me."

"Huh?" Chris reared his head back.

"You heard me. Your wife is scared to death. She was smart enough to come to me for help, something your dumb ass should have done."

Chris was furious. How could Misty go behind his back? He looked at Mister. "What do you plan on doing? How the fuck can you help? It's the fucking Russian mafia, and you're a detective from fucking McKeesport. You can't go across the bridge and arrest someone, let alone help me."

"If that's how you feel, son. I give you too much credit. I thought you were smarter than that," Mister replied.

"What are you going to do, arrest them?" Chris asked, laughing.

"Maybe if you would have come to me first you would have realized that even though I'm a cop, I'm still a friend. I can help you, Chris. I can get you out of this, but you gotta work with me."

"Work with you? I ain't no fucking rat!"

Mister cut him off. "Motherfucker, I didn't ask you to be no rat. If you would shut the fuck up and listen I'll tell your stupid ass."

Chris took a seat on a stepladder and listened to Country's dad. When he finished, Chris stared at him. "I'd have to start over again. I'm tired of starting over."

"Christopher, you have a beautiful family who I've already spoken to. They are willing to walk away to be with you. Walk away from everything they love. How long do you think it will be before either you get caught or die? Son, the devil don't show no mercy. As long as you allow him to feed your desires you are his slave, indebted to him. You have to walk away."

Chris tried to consider another option. The anger toward Misty had subsided, and he realized his wife was trying to save her family. Mister needed an answer, and Chris gave it to him.

"Okay. I'll do it."

"I know it's hard, but you're doing the right thing. Go get Misty and her mother and meet me at this address tonight at seven," Mister said as he grabbed a notepad and pencil off Chris's workbench and wrote it down.

Chris nodded and took the paper. Without another word, Mister turned and left.

CHAPTER 40

I t was seven on the dot when Chris pulled into the small home in North Hills. He noticed Mister's truck in the driveway and got out of the car. As Misty, Autumn, and her mother Beverly, who was holding David joined them, Mister opened the front door to the house and welcomed them in.

The home was a modest, two bedroom brick home. Upon entering, it reminded him of his grandmother's home. The furniture was twenty years old and worn, but clean. The carpet was a burnt orange and at one time may have been fashionable.

Mister led them through the home to the smaller bedroom that was situated at the end of the hallway. The room was set up as an office with a large metal desk with a computer monitor and stacks of papers. Behind the desk were shelves of dusty books. To the right of the door was a couch, and the next wall had a worktable with another computer, a printer, and a laminator. Sitting at the desk was a large white man in sweatpants and a wrinkled T-shirt. He wore his long black hair pulled back in a ponytail.

"Wesley, this is Christopher and his family. Chris, this is Wes," Mister said.

Wesley nodded and continued to work. He finally turned around, removed his wire-rimmed glasses, and offered his hand. "Nice to meet you."

Chris shook his hand. "Same here."

Over the next two hours, Wesley took pictures, printed information, and packaged all the necessary paper work for Chris and his loved ones to start a new life. While they waited, Mister told Chris that Wesley and he were in Vietnam together. They stayed close throughout the years, even though Wesley had chosen a path that wasn't exactly legal.

When Wesley was finished, he sat everyone down and went over the legal documents that would withstand any check. Chris and Misty were now Gary and Samantha Hatcher. Misty's mother was Stephanie Perez. The identification belonged to people who were recently deceased. It would be used to purchase homes, to get work, or any transaction that would allow them to be traced. They could use their own names for everyday life, but the less they used them the better.

Misty stood to lose the most. Her dream of teaching was gone. She no longer would be able to use her degree, but her family was more important.

They all decided that San Diego would be their new home. Misty's mother told them how beautiful it was. Chris and Misty spent hours on the Internet doing their research earlier that day. She and her mother Beverly had already decided anyway, but Chris was fine with it.

As they left Wesley's home, Chris thanked him and asked how much he owed.

"Some deeds are priceless," Wesley replied.

Mister walked Chris to the car.

"You okay?" asked Mister.

"I'm fine. A little nervous, but nothing I can't handle."

"When you leaving?"

"I got three weeks before I go see the Russian. I don't have any more coke. I just need to pick up this money, so I can at least have someone pay him. I hope if I don't owe they won't bother to look for me."

"Is that safe? To give their money to someone else?"

Chris prayed it was. He prayed that Alex would be forced to give Gabe a chance. That Gabe would do right and that the Russians would forget about him.

"I think so," Chris replied.

With all that said, the two men embraced and then went their separate ways.

CHAPTER 41

On the last day of February, Alex pulled into Immaculate Detail and made his way inside. Upon entering, he was greeted by Gabe and his expression turned sour. Chris had been warned. Alex didn't trust nor did he like Gabe, whom he saw as only a flashy street thug. Chris had been told that Alex didn't want to see anyone else.

"Where is Chris?" Alex asked, clearly upset.

"He ain't here," Gabe said.

"Well, when will he be?"

"Chris is gone. He's not coming back, but your money is in them duffle bags on the table. From now on you'll have to deal with me."

Chris told Gabe to give Alexander his money and tell him that Chris had disappeared. Chris emphasized that Gabe shouldn't approach Alex about doing business, but Gabe didn't listen. Alex's face became red as his jaw tightened.

"Who do you think you're talking to you black monkey? You give me an order. I have to deal with you? You fucking peasant. Where is Chris?"

"Monkey! Pussy, Chris might have been scared of you, but I'm not. I'll take your money and bag your punk ass," Gabe said as he reached into his waistband to grab his .40 caliber

Glock. He began to raise it, but he wasn't quick enough for the Russian. Two shots exploded, shredding Gabe's hand that held the gun. Pain shot through his arm as he fell to one knee.

Alexander Jacovich was not an ordinary thug. He had a military background, having served as a soldier in Russia's elite Spetsnaz GRU, the Russian version of Special Forces. However, the lure of money and power that the mafia had to offer enticed Alex. He spoke softly to Gabe.

"You've made this very hard on yourself. The threats I made to Chris were baseless. He would have not been worth my time to track down, but your actions have turned a business transaction into something more personal. You're gonna die, but how you go is up to you." Alex raised the pistol to Gabe's head and asked, "Where the fuck is he?"

"Fuck you!" Gabe spat.

The gun popped and Gabe clutched his left leg as the projective tore through his flesh.

"Motherfucker!" Gabe hollered as the gun sounded again, this time tearing through his right leg.

Alexander transformed into that same devil that visited him during his time in the mountains of Afghanistan, and one of his enemies begged for mercy. The flashback brought out all his suppressed evil. He walked over to a workbench and retrieved a large wrench and a torch. Lighting the torch and holding the wrench with a shop rag, he ran the blue flame over it. Gabe couldn't run. He watched in wide-eyed horror.

"I'm going to ask you again. Where did he go?"

Gabe didn't answer. He couldn't answer if he wanted to. Over the next hour, Alex tortured Gabe, burning his flesh as it sizzled and darkened. He stripped him out of his clothes and sodomized him with the end of the torch. Finally, the propane in the torch ran out. Gabe lay on the concrete floor a desecrated mess. The torch had burnt away his flesh and left deep pockets all over him. He had been dead for a while, but Alex was relentless, being driven by a deeper force. As if overcome with sudden peace, Alex dusted off his clothes, grabbed his duffel bags and left. Before leaving, Alex spoke aloud, "I'm gonna find you, Chris. And when I do, you are gonna pay for this mess."

CHAPTER 42

I t was a perfect day. Five years had passed, and Chris was on the other side of the county. He drove past Mission Bay as he rolled down the highway on his way home. Misty and her mother had their reasons for choosing San Diego. Chris found out that Rico had grown up here. Misty's cousins, aunts and uncles still resided here. For the first few years, Chris had looked over his shoulder, peering into the shadows and waiting for the devil to come collect his due. However, time passed and so did the paranoia. Chris was living a normal life. His home was in the name of Gary Hatcher. His new Ford F150 was in his own name. He sold the detail shop to a friend of Mister's after Gabe's death. He maintained a Pennsylvania address with a post office box. Once a month Mister would mail its contents. The Pennsylvania address allowed Chris to maintain a valid license without revealing his whereabouts. He had only been back to Pennsylvania once. It was then that he sold his BMW and opted for the modest truck. Life was good. Autumn had just turned fourteen. She was in middle school, and the boys were starting to show interest. Chris wanted to kill them, but Misty kept him in line.

For money, Chris invested in a small restaurant with Misty's cousin in San Diego's gas lamp quarter. It turned out to be very profitable, and Chris and his family lived well.

THE DEVIL'S GAME

Chris turned onto his street smiling until he noticed the black Cadillac CTS sitting in his driveway. The car was brand new, and Chris knew it didn't belong. Chris's truck was barely in park as he threw the door open and ran inside. In seconds, the front door was open and Chris was standing in his living room.

On the couch were Misty and a man whom Chris would never forget. The man was playing with David, when he looked up and spoke.

"Hello Christopher. Remember me?"

CPSIA information can be obtained at www.ICGtesting.com
Printed in the USA
LVOW04s2126120914

403915LV00009B/87/P

9 781936 649310